Blackbone 3

-A Novel Written by-
Caryn Lee

Copyright © 2014 by True Glory Publications
Published by True Glory Publications LLC

Facebook: Caryn Lee
Twitter: @CarynDLee
Instagram: @authorcarynlee

This novel is a work of fiction. Any resemblances to actual events, real people, living or dead, organizations, establishments or locales are products of the author's imagination. Other names, characters, places, and incidents are used fictitiously.

Cover Design: Michael Horne
Editor: Kylar Bradshaw

Because of the dynamic nature of the Internet, any Web addresses or links contained in this book may have changed since publication, and may no longer be valid. The views expressed in this work are solely those of the author and do not necessarily reflect the views of the publisher and the publisher hereby disclaims any responsibility for them.

Acknowledgements

I would like to thank God for everything. You have opened doors for me that I never even imagined were there to be opened. Thank you for opening up my eyes and allowing me to see a vision that I didn't know was there. I praise you for that. Even though I fall short of giving You the glory, You continue to prove that You are all I need. I would like to thank my family and friends.

I would like to thank my literary team True Glory Publications.

I would like to thank Author Teresa D Patterson for such a wonderful "Writer Wednesday" interview. Also Pen'Ashe Magazine for posting "Blackbone" in your "Readers Corner."

Last but not least I would LOVE to thank all of my readers that showed me love and gave me support. Thank you for taking this road trip with me as I wrote the "Blackbone Series." Thank you for buying my book, spreading the word and shouting me out on your pages. Thank you for reaching out to me on social media, for your reviews and for supporting me. Now, it's my time to return the favor and shout you out! (In no particular order.)T hank you Da Blackbone Ceo, Sharon Bell, Eyeliza Conner, Shalonda Young, Octavia Tai Willard, DeShanna Kyles, Jessica Denton, Nicole Greenhoward, Bri Auna, Latasha Richardson Edwards, Vee Singlelady Cody, Chemona Taylor, June Gordon, Amber Smith, April G. Rose, Lynn Y. Lewis, Anita Johnson Evans, Darrineka Lacy, Pearle Johns, ReNee Green, Sophia Holt, Vurina Lee, Veronica Teagus, Traci Dyre, Maegan McNeil, Kia Harrell, Nikki

Williams, Belinda Payne, Shamonica Stone, Shandriel Guilbeaux, Angela Corum, Laurie Thomas, Ashley Smith and Niki Jilvontae. Please don't kill me if I left anyone out. I truly appreciate each and every one of you. Thank You! Thank You! Thank You & Please Enjoy!

Table of Contents

Blackbone 3

By: Caryn Lee

Chapter One

Ciara

I jumped out of my sleep. I was having a nightmare once again. Ever since the death of Rochelle's, I've been having all types of crazy nightmares. I feel like the bitch is coming back to haunt me on purpose. I secretly pop pills before I go to sleep at night in hopes of a peaceful sleep. The pills didn't work so I started drinking a glass of wine right before bed, but that failed as well. I jumped out of bed and Smooth grabbed my arm.

"Where are you going baby?" he asked.

I snatched my arm away angrily, "I'm going down stairs to grab a glass of water," I said with an attitude.

"Hurry back upstairs," he mumbled in his sleepy voice.

I slid on my house shoes and satin robe. I made it downstairs grabbed me a glass, turned on the water to rinse off the glass. Fuck drinking a glass of water I needed something stronger to deal with everything that is going on inside me. I put a few ice cubes in my glass and walked over to Smooth's bar and grabbed the bottle of Patron. I poured myself a glass and drank it quickly. My chest was burning inside. I'm not a drinker and I promised that I would never drink after seeing what alcohol did to my mother. I broke that promise and didn't care. The alcohol took all the pain away and made me feel numb to all the bullshit that was going on. I know that I hated Rochelle, but I didn't want her dead. After she was shot and killed in front of her daughter and my wedding guests on my wedding day, I stood over her lifeless body crying as I watched her take her last breath. I felt sorry for her and most of all I felt sorry for Erica. I was so angry with Smooth because if he would've kept his dick in his pants like he was supposed to I wouldn't have to go through all this bullshit. I drank two more glasses of Patron. I was feeling really good inside. I was tipsy and walked upstairs. I stopped in Eric Jr. room and he was asleep with one hand down his pull up. I smiled and thought just like his damn daddy. I checked on Erica and she was asleep as well. I walked over to her and kissed her softly on her forehead trying not to wake her. A smile spread across her face as if she was aware that I just kissed her. I walked out and went back in my bedroom. Smooth was sleeping. I lay down in bed and looked up at my ceiling. I wish that I could make it all go away. Smooth rolled over and kissed me on the neck.

"What took you so long baby?" he asked.

I lay there quietly. I didn't feel like talking or being bothered with him. The only reason why he's still in this house is because of the children. If it wasn't for Erica losing her mother, I would've left with Eric Jr. and said fuck Smooth. But I thought about his daughter and how she needed a woman to raise her. I know that I could never replace her

3

mother, but I would never ever make her feel as she wasn't loved or appreciated. Smooth couldn't give her that mothers touch and love. He rubbed on my pussy and I pushed his hand away. His hand worked back over toward my thighs. I turned abruptly with my back facing him. Smooth forcefully grabbed me so that I could face him. I tried to pull away from him.

"Stop playing with me Ciara." he said.

"I'm not playing with you Smooth! Do not fucking touch me! Keep your hands to yourself!" I yelled in his face.

"Have you been drinking? I smell Patron all on your breath. Ciara you don't drink. Why the fuck are you drinking?"

"Smooth you know damn well why the hell I'm drinking! Please stop acting like a month ago that your baby mother wasn't shot to death in front of her daughter and everyone else during our wedding!"

"Baby, I know, but Rochelle is at peace now. Why can't we be at peace as well?" said Smooth.

"Just because she's dead doesn't mean that she is at peace. It doesn't change the situation. We went from one bad situation to the next. Do you know how that could've turned out? You could've lost me as well. Don't forget she had the gun pointed at my head. I keep having nightmares so the drinking helps me Smooth. It makes me feel better."

Smooth held me in his arms as I cried. I tried fighting him off of me. I punched him several times, but my small fist didn't do anything. I was tipsy and my punches were no good as I missed Smooth several times swinging in the air. I gave up and buried my head in his chest. He planted soft kisses on my forehead.

"I'm sorry Ciara baby. I didn't mean to cause all of this drama and confusion. You drinking

5

isn't going to change anything. Promise me that you will stop drinking."

I promised him that I would stop drinking. Smooth laid me down and started kissing and sucking on the side of my neck. He was hitting my spot and it felt good. It's been a month since we've had sex. My clit jumped as he worked his way down to my belly button. When he parted my thighs, my heart raced. He looked up and said to me, "I love you, Ciara." before he buried his face into my pussy kissing and sucking on my lips. Our bodies twist and turned in ecstasy. I moaned in pleasure and pushed his head in further. Smooth opened up my vagina and gently flicked my clit with his tongue. I arched my back so that he could taste all of me. My eyes rolled to the back of my head as a month's worth of cum flowed out of me and Smooth licked it all.

I woke up to the smell of breakfast cooking. I popped me a pain pill because my head was banging. Three glasses of Patron was too much for a rookie. I jumped in the shower and let the water fall down on me. I washed my body with my lavender scent body wash. It helped take my headache away. I got out and wrapped my Malaysian hair up in a towel and put in my terry cloth robe. I oiled up my body and brushed my teeth. Once I was done, I walked down stairs and followed the aroma of coffee. Smooth, Erica, and Eric Jr. were sitting at the table surrounded with food. It was French toast, turkey sausage patties and links, hash browns, scrambled eggs, fresh fruit, orange juice, and coffee.

"Good morning." I said.

Erica and Eric Jr. ran over to me.

"Mommy, we made you breakfast." Erica said

"Oh, I'm so happy that you all cooked for me," I said as I bent down to kiss and hug them both. Smooth walked over to join us and I kissed and thanked him. He pulled me in closer and gave me a deeper kiss. I playfully hit him and the children started laughing. We sat down, prayed over the food, and enjoyed our breakfast. For the first time in a month, we felt like a family again.

I was upstairs in my bathroom blow drying my hair. I didn't hear when Smooth walked in on me. I turned off the blow dryer and sat it down. He wrapped his arms around me. We both stared in the mirror at one another before we spoke.

"I love you Ciara," Smooth said as he kissed my neck softly.

"I love you too Smooth," I said and faced him, "Did you hear Erica call me mommy earlier?"

"Yes I did," Smooth said.

"That was her first time ever calling me mommy. That was so out of the normal. Do you think that she is okay with her mother's death?" I asked.

"Ciara, Erica is fine. I had a talk with her and explained to her that her mother is no longer here and is in heaven," Smooth said.

"Smooth did you tell her to call me mommy?" I asked.

"No. Why would I do something like that? She felt like calling you mommy all on her own," Smooth said as he started kissing me.

I stopped him from kissing me. "Where are the children?" I asked.

"They are downstairs in the family room watching cartoons," Smooth said and went back to kissing me. I stopped him again and went to grab my curling irons so that I could curl my hair. "Smooth, you can't leave them downstairs alone," I said as I walked past him into the bathroom to plug up the curlers.

"Where are you going today?" Smooth asked.

"I'm hanging out with Kelly today. We are having a girl's day," I said.

"Okay if you need some money just grab some out of the safe. I'm going back downstairs to

9

watch television with the children. We might just hang out today. I want to take them to Pump It Up and have pizza," Smooth said.

"That sounds like fun. I'm quite sure they would enjoy that," I said and gave him a kiss. He left out the room to go back downstairs. I curled my hair in big bouncy curls and took my big paddle brush to separate the curls. I slipped on my underwear and took out a Juicy Couture jogging suit to put on. I called Kelly to let her know that I was on my way.

"Hello Kelly, I hope that you're ready girl because I'm on my way out the door," I said.

"I'm almost ready sis. I'm putting on my clothes now. Thanks to Ant for throwing me off track," Kelly said.

"Girl tell Ant that you would give him some coochie when you get back," I laughed.

Kelly yelled to Ant repeating what I said. I heard him say something in the background while laughing.

"Ciara, he said I'm just too irresistible," Kelly said laughing.

"Girl bye, anyway, I will be leaving out in twenty minutes. I will call you when I'm out front," I said.

"Okay see you in a few," Kelly said and hung up the phone.

I put on my jogging suit and gym shoes. I sprayed on some perfume and looked at myself in the mirror checking myself out. I applied some Mac lip gloss on my lips and I was good to go. I went in the safe to grab five thousand dollars just a little something for today. When I got downstairs, Smooth and the children were watching the Lego Movie. Erica and Eric Jr. stopped watching the movie to look at me.

"Mommy, where you going?" They both asked.

"Mommy is going to hang out with Aunt Kelly today," I said.

"Daddy is taking us to Pump It Up today," Erica said.

"That's good and I want you two to be on your best behavior. And Erica keep an eye on your little brother when you two out there playing around other children," I said.

"Okay, I'm the big sister. I won't let nobody hurt my little brother," Erica said.

I kissed them both and told them how much I loved them. I grabbed my purse and was headed toward the door.

"Where my kiss at?" Smooth asked.

I playfully blew him a kiss and laughed. "You better come and give me a kiss," Smooth said and grabbed me by my waist. We kissed one another and then he grabbed my ass.

"See that's why I didn't want to give you a kiss," I said.

"Baby, you look so juicy. I just had to grab it," Smooth said.

"I love you babe and Smooth keep you better not let anything happen to my babies out there," I said as I headed out the door.

"I got everything under control. You enjoy yourself and tell Kelly I said what's up," Smooth said.

I left out the house and jumped in my car in route to pick up Kelly.

Chapter Two

Kayla

I was in the recreational room playing cards with one of the other inmates named Cherish. She was the only inmate that I really talk to in here. We both had something in common; we were both pregnant and locked up serving time for the men that we loved. Once it was confirmed that I was pregnant, they moved me to the pregnancy unit. It made twenty pregnant inmates in our unit. We each had our own cell. My first day on the unit was a long boring one. I pretty much just read my book. The unit was quiet and I appreciated that. The other good thing was the pregnant inmates had to attend childbirth educational classes and group therapy sessions in Parenting, Substance Abuse, Domestic Violence, Prenatal Care, and Postpartum. That was cool because this was my first pregnancy and I didn't know what to do. I was afraid to go through the experience alone. That is how I grew close to Cherish. During one of our classes, she confessed that she was sexually molested by her mother's boyfriend. I sat back and listened to the other inmates tell their business. I was a private person and didn't feel comfortable sharing my business with strangers. After the meeting, I approached Cherish and started a conversation with her.

"Hello Cherish I'm Kayla. I was listening to you tell your story today and I wanted to tell you that we both have something in common," I said.

"Hey Kayla, I thought that you didn't talk at all. You never say much in the group. I take it that you have been molested as well?" Cherish said.

"I don't really talk that much. I'm pretty much a private person and yes I was molested by my grandfather. He molested my mother when she was younger too. Years later he started molested me," I told Cherish.

"Wow, that's deep. How did you find out about him molesting your mom? If you don't mind me asking, where was your mother when during your molestation?" Cherish asked.

15

"My mother and I lived together on the Westside of Chicago. He stayed in Indiana. My mother told me that he molested her during her childhood. My grandfather tried several times to reach out to us, but she kept him away from me and made me promise to stay away from him. My grandfather had money and we didn't have money. My mother collected SSI and had Section 8 housing. So he was able to suck me in through money and gifts. He took my virginity and we had sex multiple times. I never told anyone. One day my mother caught me sucking his dick in the car and shot and killed him then she turned around and killed herself," I cried as I shared a piece of my past with Cherish.

"Oh my Kayla, I'm so sorry that you had to experience all of that," said Cherish.

She got up and hugged me. For the first time, I shared my story with another female. The only female that I would consider a friend and someone that I trust is Aaliyah and she doesn't know about me being molested. Smooth is the only person that I've shared my secrets with and hasn't judged me. At first, he thought that I was crazy. But once I shared my past with him, he felt that I was damaged and understood why I did the things that I did for money. That was the only way that I learned. Cherish and I were both crying as we both hugged one another. The other inmates were watching us from a distance. They all looked concerned, but didn't want to ask out of fear of getting cursed out. Our little baby bumps touched one another as we hugged. Cherish grabbed her stomach suddenly and smiled.

"She's kicking," Cherish said holding her hand across her pregnant belly. I placed my hand on her belly and her baby was kicking like crazy. We both laughed until she finally stops kicking. "I guess she doesn't like me crying," Cherish said.

"When are you due?" I asked.

"My baby is due March 17th. I'm scheduled to be released in July of this year," Cherish said.

"Wow that is so crazy and funny. My due date is April 6th. I get out in August of this year," I said.

"It's fucked up that we both have to have our babies in here," Cherish said.

"Yes, real fucked up. This is my first pregnancy and I have to experience it like this," I said.

"Well this isn't my first time being pregnant. I've been pregnant twice by my man Lorenzo and both times I secretly got abortions. If I wasn't locked up and found out this time around, I would've gotten a third abortion," Cherish said.

"I know how you feel as soon as I found out that I was pregnant I tried to kill my baby girl Variyah several times. I didn't want to have any children," I said.

"Variyah, that's a pretty name for a girl and it's different. I don't have a name yet. I'm still trying to choose one," Cherish said.

"Thank you and don't worry we will think of a name. We still have plenty of time to. If you don't mind me asking, but what are you in here for?" I asked.

"No it's cool. I'm here for writing bad checks. I'm into scamming. You know credit, debit, and gift cards. I'm good at getting people social security number and bank account information. What are you in here for?" Cherish asked.

"They raided my place and found some guns and cash. I took the time," I said.

"Okay, I see and you're doing your guy time? If you don't mind me asking, what's your guy name?" Cherish said.

"My man name is Smooth. Do you know a Smooth from out west?" I asked.

"No I don't. I'm from the south side," Cherish said.

From that day forth, Cherish and I formed a bond. We talked about everything and promised to have our daughters grow up like sisters. I came up with the name Laniyah for her baby girl and she loved it. We also made plans to get money together once we both got out of this place. Cherish was already teaching me some of the scamming techniques. It was pretty easy and besides I was about getting money. I know that Smooth promised me that he had everything covered, but I still had to make my own money. With him dealing with Ciara, he wasn't officially mine. But with me having his child, that was guaranteed income that covered a roof over my head, food, in the house, and weekly money for Variyah. Aaliyah had told me everything that had happened at his wedding. I'm glad that the crazy bitch Rochelle was dead. I still think till this day that she was the one who dropped the dime on me. It was strange that after we had that altercation at my house the people kicked my doors in. When I get out, I should go and shit on that bitch's grave. It's cool because now that she's out of the picture I can go toe to toe with this bitch Ciara. She doesn't have a clue that I'm pregnant. She knows that I'm locked up for her man though. I hope that she enjoys the happiness while she can because when I get out it's about me and my baby, and the bitch is going to have to deal with it. I'm not keeping anything on low or hiding like that dead bitch did. I continued to play cards with Cherish when the guard told me that I had a visitor. I got up and made sure that I was appropriate. When I got downstairs, Aaliyah was waiting to see me. We both hugged and embraced one another. It was good to get a visit from someone and to know that someone cared. I sat down and we started to talk.

"What's up baby mama? How's my God baby doing?" Aaliyah asked.

"Everything is going fine. I have my monthly doctor appointment next week. I can't wait. That's the good thing about being pregnant and locked up is that we get to go out for our doctor appointments," I said.

"That's good I was going to tell you that I was going to visit you during our last phone call, but I thought that I'd surprise you instead," Aaliyah said laughing.

"Girl, you can come up here anytime. I need the visits," I said.

"So what you been doing in here? Smooth told me to tell you that he hasn't forgotten about you and that he received your letter that you sent him on Coorlinks," Aaliyah said.

"Girl just going to parenting classes and shit I met another pregnant inmate in here named Cherish she cool. Other than that, I'm just serving my time and reading. I know that Smooth is dealing with the death of that crazy bitch. You have to finish telling me what happened," I said.

"Kayla, it was crazy. She just popped out in the aisle of the church pointing the gun at Ciara. A few people sat there and watched, and some ran. Those who remained got low and ducked. She was crying and told Ciara that she wanted her daughter back and how she hated her for fucking up her life. She pulled the trigger, but missed Ciara. Next thing you know someone else shot her and she dropped to the floor and died. Right in front of her daughter it was so sad," Aaliyah said.

"Wow, what did Ciara do after that?" I asked.

"I don't know me and Vell left after that, but I heard that she sat there and cried," Aaliyah said.

"I feel bad for Smooth's daughter to have to witness all of that. I know how she feels; I can empathize with her because when I was younger I witnessed my mother take her own life," I said.

"What Kayla? I've never known that. I'm sorry to hear that. You never shared that with me," Aaliyah said.

"It's a lot you don't know about my past, but right now, I just want to focus on my future and have a healthy baby girl. Rochelle didn't kill Ciara; but once she finds out about my baby, I know for sure that she's going to die or try to kill herself," I said.

Aaliyah and I sat there and talked for the next thirty minutes until our visit was up. I was so happy that she came to see me and kept me updated on everything. I wished that Smooth would come and visit me, but due to the situation he told me that it was best that he didn't. I missed him so much and I can't wait till I get out. I asked the guards could I make a phone call and they allowed me to. I went to call Smooth. He answered and I heard a lot of children in the background.

"Hello, hey bae, I miss you. I'm so happy that you picked up," I said.

"What's up Kayla? I'm so sorry about not being in contact with you, but it's been a lot of bullshit going on," Smooth said.

24

"It's cool I understand. I got the money that you sent me too. Aaliyah just left from up here," I said.

"Oh yeah, that's good. Aaliyah cool as hell. I'm happy that the two of you formed a friendship," Smooth said.

"Yes, I want her and Vell to be the God parents of our child," I said.

"That can be arranged that's not a problem. Wait, hold on, let me see what Eric Jr. is doing," Smooth said.

He put me on hold for a minute and I could hear him in the background talking to Eric Jr. and Erica. I don't know where he was, but you can hear a lot of children in the background. I assumed that he was out with the children. I wonder if Ciara was with him. He got back on the phone.

"My fault Kayla I'm at Pump It Up with the kids. Eric Jr. was pushing on another little boy. I had to see what the hell was going on," Smooth said.

I laughed imagining Eric Jr. pushing another boy. From what he just told me, I don't think that Ciara is with him. I didn't want to ask him about her because it was about me right now.

"It's cool. I hope that I didn't call you at a bad time," I said.

"No you good. How is my baby doing? Are you taking the prenatal vitamins that the doctor prescribed you? Are you eating well?" Smooth asked.

"The baby is doing great. I'm taking my prenatal vitamins and with the money that you sent me I'm eating well," I said.

"Okay let me know if you need anything else Kayla. I'm about to get off this phone and keep an eye on my kids. You hang in there. It would be over with soon," Smooth said.

"I know I can't wait till it's over. I miss you and can't wait till you see you again," I said as I began to cry.

"Kayla don't cry everything is going to be alright. I got you as soon as you get out. I promise and I love you girl," Smooth said.

"I love you too, Smooth and you promise you going to be there for me?" I asked.

"Yes, I'm here for you now. Don't worry, I got you," Smooth said.

The guard gave me the signal letting me know that my time was up. I stuck up my index finger indicating one minute. She nodded her head.

"Okay Smooth, I believe you. My time is up now and I have to go to my cell. I will call you tomorrow. I love you Smooth," I said.

"I love you too Kayla. I'll holler at you tomorrow," Smooth said.

The guards walked me back to my cell. I laid down on the bunk and cried myself asleep.

Chapter Three

Kelly

Ciara was on her way to pick me up from my place. I could've driven my own car, but I wanted to hang out with my best friend just like the old days. It's been a month since the incident and everything that had occurred. I was happy that my best friend decided to put that behind her. I wasn't happy with the fact that Smooth had put Ciara in that position to deal with that crazy bitch. And to think I thought Ebony was crazy. Speaking of her, we both still had some unfinished business to settle. She ran her scary ass out of town. She didn't even attend her own father's funeral. I'm sure one that she would pop back up in Chicago. I heard that she was down in Texas. I'm not going to worry about her; we will meet again. I sprayed some oil sheen on my hair for the finished touch. Since Jasmine's death, me and Ciara have been going to a new hairstylist named Ryan. He was a young gay, black male that was cold on the hairstyles. I was rocking a bob with a side bang over my eye. Ryan was great with razor cut. That is was made me fall in love with him. I miss my sis Jasmine so much though. She appeared in my dream the other night. I have to tell Ciara about it today. My phone rang and I knew that it was her out front. My cell phone was on the table in the dining room. Ant came walking in the bedroom talking to Ciara on my phone before he handed it to me.

"I'm ready. I'm ready. I will be out in one minute," I said.

I slipped on my gym shoes and grabbed my leather black crop jacket. It was fall in Chicago. I walked in the living room where Ant was playing the Xbox.

"Babe, I will be back this evening," I said.

"Where are you going, bae? Give me a kiss," Ant said.

"We're going to Woodfield Mall and after that grabbing a bite to eat," I said before giving him a kiss.

"Okay be safe out there and when I call you make sure that you answer your phone," Ant said.

"Since when haven't I answered my phone when you called me Ant?" I asked.

"Never and you better stop getting sassy by mouth," Ant said while he smacked me on my ass.

I kissed him on the lips, "You love my sassy mouth. I love you and I will answer when you call," I said before leaving out the door. When I jumped in the car, Ciara was looking at me with a smirk on her face. "What? I was ready blame Ant," I laughed jokily. We both started laughing hard before Ciara pulled off. As we rode to the mall, I asked about the children. She said that they were at home with Smooth and hanging out with him for the day. Chris Brown song came on, "Loyal," and she turned it up. We sang and listened to the song and when it went off Ciara played it again.

"Wow isn't we feeling some type of way today I see," I said.

"Girl yes I am. All the bullshit that nigga Smooth put me through. This song is perfect for his ass," Ciara said.

"Yes, especially Lil Wayne part. Why give a bitch your heart when she'd rather have a purse. Girl that shit reminds me of Ebony's ass," I said.

"Kelly these niggas don't care. They like fucking with hoes," Ciara said.

I sat back and listened to Ciara talk. I knew that she was still harboring some pain inside. It was hard when she found out about Smooth and his love child. She never really could get over that. I tip my head off to her for sticking by her man and for allowing his love child to live with them. If it was me, I couldn't do it. I know that Ant and I had our situation with Ebony, but when he fucked her me

32

and Ant wasn't serious. I didn't have a problem with him having a questionable baby on the way. I had a problem with that hoe Ebony because she kept on fucking with me. Now, Ciara and Smooth's situation was different. He cheated on Ciara and got Rochelle pregnant. Then he hid a baby. What type of real man does that? Ciara gets pregnant and he was still fucking the other crazy bitch and then coming home to fuck his girl. That's too much bullshit to handle. To be honest, I can't stand Smooth's ass anymore. Every time he speaks to me, I don't say anything. I hold grudges and I really want to fuck him up, but that's my girl man and her business. Plus he's Ant's friend as well so I just keep it peaceful. I love my best friend with all my heart, but I don't want to end up like her. That's why I wear my heart on my sleeve. Don't get me wrong I love Ant, but I'm not accepting no other child period that you made while you were fucking with me. I love myself more. After I fuck him up and the side bitch too, I would have just moved on after that. We made it to Woodfield Mall and searched for a parking spot. It was Saturday morning and crowded. We shopped for the kids first and got them out of the way. Next, we shopped for ourselves and I grabbed me a few pair of jeans, sweaters, and a pair of boots. It was my third year at Chicago State University. My goal was to be a real estate agent and to own my own company as well. After this, I want to enroll into the University of Chicago, but my brother Shawn wanted me to finish school in California. I've been talking to him a lot lately and I and Ant planned on going to see him on my spring break. Ant wasn't too thrilled about me moving to Cali. Shawn spoke with him and told him that money was sweet in Cali and that he wanted to do business with him. I didn't get involved when it came to Ant's business, so I stayed out of it. Honestly, I didn't want to move to Cali, but I didn't want to stay in Chicago either. Ant and I would discuss that when the time is right. My phone rang and it was Ant calling me for the third time since I've been at the mall. Ciara laughed and that it was cute. I didn't it was irritating as hell.

"Girl that's love he just showing you how much he missed you," Ciara said.

"That's fine, but do he have to call me every hour like I am a child," I said.

"Smooth only called me once since we've been out," Ciara said.

"Ciara please just because Smooth called you once that doesn't mean he loves you any less than Ant loving me," I said.

"All I'm saying is Kelly quit bitching and be happy, it could be worse," Ciara said while trying on a pair of boots.

"Whatever," I said rolling my eyes.

After we were finished shopping we went to Maggiano's to sit down and eat. I was starving so I ordered my favorite Chicken Marsala and Ciara ordered Chicken & Spinach Manicotti and a glass of wine. We ate our food and talked. When our waiter came over to ask if everything was okay, Ciara ordered another glass of wine. I looked at her in shocked and she looked at me like what.

"Ciara what the hell are you doing? You know you don't drink," I said being concerned.

"I'm just having a glass of wine. Kelly what the fuck is the big deal?" Ciara said.

"The big deal is that you don't fucking drink at all Ciara and now you throwing that wine back like you're at the last supper," I said.

"Girl, what the fuck else am I supposed to do!" Ciara yelled causing a scene.

I know this heifer didn't just yell at me. It was time for us to go. I signaled for the waiter and he came over.

"We're ready for the bill please," I said.

The waiter returned with the bill and I paid for our meals. We exited the restaurant quietly as

36

the patrons watched us. I was so embarrassed. When we reached Ciara's car, I snatched the keys out of her hand and drove. Ciara didn't say anything; she got inside the car and quietly looked outside the window. I guess she didn't want to look at me or talk. I didn't have time to play games. I was about to give it to her straight with no chaser since she wants to start drinking now.

"Ciara, I know that you've been through a lot, but drinking isn't going to make the pain go away. You turning to the wrong thing for help and I'm surprised at you because this isn't the person that I know. You of all people know what alcohol abuse can to do people and I know that you don't want to be like the type of mother that you had growing up. It could lead to that if you keep on drinking. You're a fighter. Hell, that's how I met you. If you ever need to talk, you have me, your mother, and God. Don't you ever let me see another drink in your hand. If I do, I'm going to smack the shit out of you and we're going to be fighting. Ciara, I love you and I don't want to lose you like we lost Jasmine," I said.

Ciara sat in the passenger seat crying. I didn't like to see my friend hurting inside. The drive back to her house was silent. When we got to Ciara's home, Smooth and the kids weren't there. I called Ant and told him that I needed to be picked up from Ciara's place and I will call him when I'm ready. He said no problem and didn't ask any questions. Ciara and I sat in the living room and I was eager to hear what she had to say.

"I'm not going anywhere, not until we talk," I said.

Ciara spoke, "Kelly, I just want to be happy. Have a happy family minus the lies and the bullshit. I just want an honest man that I can trust. Someone that I don't have to question every time he walks out the door. I feel like the love isn't there any longer and I'm just here and not living. I have to drink to lay next to him. I have to drink to forget about Rochelle's death. I have to drink to take the pain away."

"Ciara did you talk to Smooth about this? Does he know that you're drinking?" I asked.

"No and yes. Earlier this morning, we had a talk after he smelled Patron on my breath. I sneak and drink some Patron," Ciara said.

I looked over at the bar in the dining room and back at Ciara. "I understand that you want to be happy. Ciara there is going to be some bumps and bruises in life. You have to be able to overcome them and not let them overcome you," I said.

"Sometimes I just feel alone. Like I'm faking it to be happy. I feel like Smooth took a sharp knife and stabbed me in my heart. I had second thoughts on becoming his wife. I just went on with the wedding. When Rochelle interrupted our wedding, that was a sign that Smooth and I shouldn't be getting married," Ciara said.

"Do you love Smooth?" I asked.

"Yes I love Smooth without a doubt. The problem is I don't think that he loves me," Ciara said.

"If he loves you, he needs to show you that he loves you," I said.

Just when Ciara was about to say another word, Smooth and the children came through the door. Ciara and I looked at one another with looks confirming that we will finish our conversation later.

"Hey baby, how was the mall? Hey Kelly, what's up?" Smooth asked.

"Hello Smooth," I spoke very short.

Erica and Eric Jr. ran over to me screaming, "Hey auntie Kelly!"

I hugged them both. "Hey babies, I miss you. Oh my Jr. you are getting so big and Erica you're getting prettier and prettier every time I see you," I said.

I smothered them with hugs and kisses. I haven't seen them in a month. They told me about how much fun they had at Pump It Up. Smooth and Ciara went in the back to talk. While Erica and Eric Jr. showed me their cool prizes, I pulled out my phone and told Ant that I was ready to be picked up. He said he was on the way. I snapped a few selfies with the children I really missed them so much. They kept me entertained until Ciara and Smooth came back to join us. Ant called my phone and told me he was out front. Smooth went outside to holler at him. The children went to their rooms and Ciara and I was left alone.

"We're not finish with our talk. I will give you a call tomorrow once I get out of class," I said as I hugged her.

"Okay and thank you Kelly for listening," Ciara said.

"Anytime, that's what friends are for. Through good times and bad times," I said.

Ciara walked with me outside, but didn't go too far because the children were in the house alone. She waved at Ant from her porch. I walked toward the truck and Ant opened the door to let me in. Before I got in, I pulled Smooth to the side.

"Smooth can you remove the liquor from your home? I asked.

"Sure no problem," Smooth said.

I walked away and got inside the truck. Ant and Smooth talked quickly wrapping up their conversation. When Ant jumped back in the truck, he asked me what was going on. I told him that I will tell him once we made it home.

Chapter Four

Smooth

Ant and Kelly pulled off and I went back in the house with my family. I went to go get an empty box and came back in the dining room. I removed all the bottles of liquor from the bar and took the box to the garage behind the tool shed. Once I made it back in the house, I went to check on the children. Ciara was in the kitchen cooking dinner. I walked in and hugged her from behind.

"What are you making gorgeous?" I asked.

"Lasagna and garlic bread. How was Pump It Up?" Ciara asked.

"It was a lot of fun even though they kept me busy. The children really enjoyed themselves," I said.

"It's not easy. Now you see what I have to go through," Ciara laughed.

I turned her around so that she could face me. "Yes baby, it isn't easy. You're a superwoman I don't know how you do it," I said kissing her lips softly.

Ciara kissed me and wrapped her arms around my neck. My dick got hard and it poked her. She grabbed my bulging dick.

"Someone is happy to see me," she grinned.

"He's always happy to see you," I whispered in her ear.

Eric Jr. ran into the kitchen and me and Ciara jumped. He pulled me away to join him in the room to show me a wrestling move that he seen on television. Damn, he came at the wrong time. I went to the room with him to watch WWF Wrestling and wrestled with him for an hour. Ciara interrupted us to tell us that dinner was ready. Erica was in the dining room helping Ciara set the table. We all gathered at the table, prayed, and ate dinner. The children ate their food quickly. Ciara gave them both their baths and put them to bed. Once she made it to the bedroom, I could tell by the look on her face that she was exhausted. I had that covered and walked her inside our personal bathroom to the Jacuzzi where I had the water prepared for her. I undressed her and she got inside. I took the sponge and added her favorite Bath & Body Works body wash and washed her body down. Once she was done, I dried her body off and oiled her body down. Ciara laid on her stomach as I massaged her shoulders and back. I worked my hands down to her waist and her apple shaped ass. I caressed each one of her ass cheeks. The sight of her ass made my dick hard and pre cum was on tip. Ciara arched her back exposing her pretty pussy in my face. Her juicy pussy looked tasty. I slurped on her pussy as she threw her ass back covering my entire face. My tongue fucked her pussy and her sweet juices squirted out and down my throat. I entered her from the back and she tried to run. I pulled her hair and plunged my dick in her deeper. She looked back at me with a grin on her face as she took my dick and fucked me back telling me, "I love you." I couldn't hold it in much longer and unleashed myself inside her and collapsed on top of her oily body. We both didn't move. We wanted to stay in this position so I feel asleep in that pussy.

Sunday we all stayed inside and had family day. Ciara made a run to the store to buy a few things for dinner. The children and I played board games while Ciara made Sunday dinner. We were playing Chutes and Ladders. Erica got excited and accidently knocked Ciara's purse on the floor. I went to pick up her Gucci purse and I noticed that two small personal sized wines had fallen out of her purse. I quickly picked them up and stuffed them in my back pocket. I went back to playing the game with the children and decided to talk to Ciara about it later. After we ate dinner, we all watched a movie together in the living room. Thirty minutes later Erica and Eric Jr. were asleep. I took them to their bedrooms and put them in bed. Ciara and I were alone and snuggled on the couch watching the movie. I felt like it was the perfect time for me to bring up the personal sized alcohol bottles in her purse.

"Ciara baby, I thought you promised me that you would stop drinking," I said.

"I'm not drinking anymore. What are you talking about?" Ciara asked.

I went in my pocket to pull out the two bottles.

"Where did these come from?" I asked.

Ciara jumped up. "Why are you going in my purse?" she asked.

"I didn't go through your purse. Earlier today when Erica knocked your purse down by accident these fell out. So you're still drinking," I said.

"It's only wine. You know what I don't want to talk about this right now. I'm going to bed," Ciara said.

She walked upstairs to go to bed. I stayed downstairs and didn't go behind her because right now I didn't feel like arguing. Instead, I called her mother. Brenda answered the phone and by her voice I could tell that I woke her up.

"Hello Brenda, its Smooth sorry to wake you. No everyone is fine no need to worry. I hate to bother you this late, but I need to talk to you about something regarding your daughter," I said.

I explained everything to Brenda and twenty minutes later I joined Ciara in bed.

In the morning, I woke up to Ciara sucking my dick. It was so vicious that I put the pillow over my face. Once she drained me out, I got up to get in the shower. When I got out, I noticed that I had several missed calls. I called Vell back first.

"What's up Vell? What's the word?" I said.

"Nigga, we waiting on you at the spot," Vell said.

"Oh shit, give me thirty minutes," I said.

"Cool," Vell said before hanging up.

I got dressed and grabbed my pistol and placed it in my waist. I jogged down the stairs and Erica and Eric Jr. we're finishing up their breakfast. Ciara was preparing them for school. She looked radiant with her hair pulled back in a ponytail with her crop tee, skin tight jeans, and high heel pumps.

"Where do you think you're going looking this good?" I said grabbing her by the waist.

"I'm going back to work. Did you forget that I have a company to run?" Ciara said.

"You just look too good. I don't think I should let you out of my sight," I said.

She laughed as she continued to get the children and their things together to head out the door. I grabbed a sausage patty and ate it. Ciara turned off the lights and gave me a kiss. We all left out and entered the garage to get in our cars. I kissed the children and told them to have a good day in school.

"Smooth, you be careful okay. I love you," Ciara said.

"Okay baby, I love you too and tonight we need to talk," I said.

Ciara rolled her eyes because she knew what I wanted to discuss with her. She jumped behind the wheel, the garage door opened, and she pulled off. I pulled off shortly behind her and made it to the spot. Vell, Bird, and Ant was waiting along with a few more of the workers. Vell started the meeting.

"We had a great year in Chicago making more money than we could imagine. Although, we did we

49

haven't made enough to retire." There were a few laughs. "And Chicago only allows us to do so much. So we've decided to make more moves down south in Texas. We have linked up with Tommy and he's ready for us to give him the word. In Texas, we can triple our money, but we have to do it smart. I'm asking everyone to invest fifty thousand if you're down. It's all up to you. With that amount of money, we can open up shop, hire several cookers and workers, and flood enough coke in Dallas and Houston. Does anyone have in questions?" Vell said.

The room remained silent. I loved how much our team believed in one another and had loyalty and trust installed. Last year we seen a difference in our lives and that was only a few thousand. This year we had plans on seeing millions. Vell wrapped up the meeting and told everyone that we had a month to put up our share of the money and to get this thing going. I pulled Vell to the side.

"Hey let Aaliyah know that I appreciate her for going to check on Kayla this weekend," I said.

"Yeah, I see her and Kayla getting pretty close. I'm surprised because Aaliyah isn't really that open with females like that," Vell said.

"Well, you know her and Ciara never really seen eye to eye and you know Aaliyah and Kayla kind of experienced the same thing before as far as the hustling part of the game," I said.

"Yes that's true, but partner what you going to do about the baby?" Vell asked.

"Kayla is keeping it. That's what I want to holler at you about. I want Aaliyah to take the baby until she gets out. She's due to have the baby in April, but she doesn't get out until four months later in August. Kayla is going to have to give her baby to someone. Even though it's my child, I can't take my baby home with me," I said

"Well, you know you my man and I got you, but I don't know how you're going to keep this away from Ciara Bro," Vell said.

"I'll deal with that when I have to cross that bridge," I said.

"As long as you have it under control it's all good. I just don't want any problems with Ciara. She's a firecracker man and will explode on your ass," Vell said laughing.

"Man, I can handle Ciara. Trust me I got this under control," I said laughing, but deep down inside I had to figure out what the fuck I was going to do.

Chapter Five

Ciara

I went back to work running Bella Boutique. After the fire and the loss of my last boutique, I relocated and opened my new one in Oak Park. I was an upscale area and not so deep in the suburbs but not in the city. My assistant London and I was preparing to get the place up and running for my re grand opening. I had my new items in the box and was looking forward to another large shipment to come in for today. Looking out the window, I seen London pull up. I was so happy that she arrived because I needed her help. Last night when I spoke with her, she sounded like she had a cold. She came in with hair pulled back with a headband, a scarf wrapped around her neck, and a pair of jeans with some cowboy boots.

"Good morning Ciara," she said sounding hoarse.

"Good morning London. You sound bad maybe you need to take the day off. Are you sure you're well enough to work?" I asked.

"I'm fine it's just the change in the weather. I will be just fine. Besides, I couldn't leave you alone to handle all this merchandise," London said.

"Okay, I'm just making sure just keep your germs to yourself," I said laughing, but I was really serious.

"Don't worry I will. Now, let's get to work. Where are the mannequins? How many do you want displayed in the window? How are we dressing them?" she asked.

"Gone girl, that's why I hired you. You always come ready to work. The mannequins are in the back and I'm thinking about maybe we should display three in the mirror. Dress one in midi dress, the second one in a top and a pair of high waist jeans, and the third one in a jumpsuit. We can also display a few pair of boots as well," I said.

London went in the back as I opened up the boxes and unpacked the clothes, boots, and accessories. We had at least ten boxes and I was expecting more to come. I really loved my new boutique because the space was much bigger and I had two dressing rooms. London steamed the clothes before dressing them on the mannequin. We had a few people stare and ask when we were opening and I told them

54

next week. I asked London to go on my business pages that I had on Facebook and Instagram and flood the timeline and put word out about Bella Boutique re grand opening. Many customers had asked when we were opening back up and was concerned after the fire. I had a website that did great for my customers from out of town, but my shop was always busy. After three hours, London and I took a break and went to sit down and eat at Friday's close by. When we got there it was a lunch crowd so we had to wait fifteen minutes before being seated. I was happy when we finally got a table. We looked over the menu and we both ordered Buffalo wings and loaded potato skins. I also ordered a margarita. London had a cup of hot tea because of her sore throat. She looked at me with a concerned look on her face. I already knew that she was about to mention the margarita that I ordered.

"So we drinking now Ciara?" she asked.

"It's only a margarita nothing hard," I said.

London gave me a crazy look, "I know that I haven't really talked to you since your wedding. How are you holding up?" she asked.

"Right after the wedding, I was a complete wreak. I didn't want Smooth to touch me at all. I hated him and blamed him for everything. I'm feeling a little better and have worked out a few things at home. Slowly, it's getting back to normal," I said.

"After all of that it's going to take some time. I know that Rochelle was crazy, but I didn't think that she was that crazy. I really feel sorry for Erica," London said.

The waiter bought our food to the table and we began to eat. London changed the subject and told me all about her new boyfriend that she had met over the summer named Jay. You can tell that she really liked him because her faced lit up the whole time she was talking about him. She spoke him up because he called her while we were eating. I smiled and thought about the time Smooth and I met and I was once crazy about him like that. I mean don't get me wrong I love him, but after a baby momma and a daughter it's a different kind of love. We ended our lunch and went back to work. UPS delivered my shipment and we unpacked and stocked them as well. I placed the extra inventory in the back. My Smooth called to check on me and to remind me that we had to talk. To be honest, I didn't really want to talk about the wine bottles that he found in my purse. He didn't have any business going through it. Now, I can't even trust him and know that he's going to be looking around for evidence of me drinking. After Smooth called me twenty minutes later Brenda called me.

"Hello Ciara, how are you doing?" Brenda asked.

"I'm doing fine. How are you doing?" I asked.

"I'm doing great. Are you busy? Can you talk now?" she asked.

"I'm pretty busy now at the boutique. London and I are getting everything together," I said.

"Okay, I was calling to talk to you. Eric called me last night. Call me when you're free to talk." she said.

"No problem I will," I said.

"Okay, tell London I said hello and I will talk to you later Ciara, good bye," Brenda said.

"London, my mother said hello. She said hello back mom and okay I will call you later. Goodbye." I ended the call.

I rolled my eyes. I can't believe that Smooth called and told my mother about my drinking. Wait till I get home, I'm going off on his ass. He didn't have to put her in our business. We could've have handled our situation without her. I pushed that to back of my head and focused on getting my boutique in order. London could tell that something wasn't right and that I didn't really want to talk about it so she turned on some music. Three hours later, Bella Boutique was new and improved. So many people were slowing down to view the mannequins and others tapped on the window to ask if we were open. London and I passed out flyers as well so that people would be aware of the opening date. I felt like I had accomplished a lot today and decided that it was time to go home and be back at it tomorrow to start the advertising and promoting part. I closed down the boutique and told London that I would see her tomorrow. Next, I had to pick up the children from daycare. They both attended the same place. It took me thirty minutes to get to them because of the traffic. I pulled up in front of Little Folks Day Care to pick up Eric Jr. and Erica. I had just enrolled them there. The lady that owned it was a teacher and I heard that she prepared her children for school once they left from here. The daycare was downstairs and the older children were upstairs. I always picked up Erica first so I headed to the elevator. While standing at the elevator someone said, "Hey Ciara." I turned around to see who it was and it was Denise, Smooth's friend Red's girl. Denise aka Niecy is Red's girlfriend. She was pretty cool and just stayed to herself. Niecy was prissy and a showoff. She and Red haven't been together that long maybe like six months. I remember the first moment I met her we did a double date. Red was so excited about her and we were happy that he finally found someone that was that one and only girl because he always had a different one every time. We went to eat at Ron of Japan and when we got there Red and Denise was already there. When I first saw her, she was pretty and so ladylike nothing like the ratchet females he introduced us to in the past. Niecy was light brown, short, and skinny with a big booty. It didn't look right because she had small legs. Rumors has it that she had her butt done. Anyway, the reason why I say that she is a showoff because during the night she described everything about her lifestyle using a designer name. I gave her a compliment on her purse and she told me, "Thank you girl, this purse cost me thousand dollars." I thought it was cute and so I brushed her comment off. I had to burst her bubble when she tried to question me on my lifestyle. Once she found out that I ran and owned my own business, she calmed herself down. Overall she was cool and never crossed me and gave me my respect so I didn't have a problem with her. I know that she attended my wedding and I was prepared to hear the, 'I'm so sorry about what happened to your speech.' So, I had to put on my happy face.

"Hey Niecy girl. How are you?" I asked.

"Girl, I'm cool. How are you doing?" she asked.

"I'm fine just taking it one day at a time," I said.

"That's great. I didn't know that your children went here. I work here," Niecy said.

"I didn't know that. Yes both Erica and Eric Jr. just started going here," I said.

"I thought I noticed Smooth's son, but I wasn't sure what his real name was. I was going to call and ask Red, but it got so busy and I didn't get a chance," Niecy said.

"So my baby is in your class. That's great that means you can really keep an eye on him," I said.

"Yes you know that I got you. Let me go on ahead and get back to work. Ciara, please take my number," Niecy said.

I pulled out my IPhone and stored her number. Niecy told me to please call her and don't be a stranger. I promised her that I would and I meant it because Jr. was in her class, so I wanted to get pretty close with her. I picked up the both of them and headed home. When I got there, I was surprised to see that Smooth was already at home. That was good because I was ready to chew his ass up about telling my mother about my damn drinking problem. I didn't feel like she needed to know and that he and I could've handled it on our own. He went to the room and helped Erica with her school work and Jr. was occupied with them as well. I started my dinner and made chicken tacos and rice and beans. Everyone was happy that I made tacos.

I'm not trying to brag, but I make the best tacos. We ate dinner and I remained cordial, but Smooth could tell that I wanted to get something off my chest. Once we were done, we put the children to sleep and we had adult time. Smooth was trying to caress my body, but I stopped him in his tracks.

"Smooth, why you call and inform my mother that I was drinking? I felt like that is a personal matter that you and I could handle on our own. Now, she's going to be down my back every day and right now I just don't feel like all of that," I said.

"Ciara that's your mother. I felt as though she have a right to know what's going on. You know that she could help since she's already been down that road before," Smooth said.

"I'm not anything like her and I never will be. I've only had a few drinks here and there. I don't wake up drinking all day and night," Ciara said.

"Drinking isn't the problem. The problem is what is causing you to drink," Smooth said.

"Okay so let's get professional help. You and I could look for someone and start our counseling. I feel comfortable doing that. I just really hate that I have to face my mother about this whole situation," I said.

I was sitting on one side of the bed and he was sitting on the other side. It was going on eight p.m. and his cell phone started ringing. He looked at the screen and pressed the decline button on the phone. I don't know why he did it, but as soon as he went to bed I was going through his phone. We got in the shower and had sex. Smooth had me hanging from the shower rod as I screamed his name. After that we went to bed and Smooth fell asleep and I pretending like I was sleeping. Once I knew that he was in a deep sleep, I went through his phone. My silly ass grabbed his index finger to unlock his phone. I smiled when it worked on the second try. My smile disappeared once I seen that his ass had erased everything in his phone. It wasn't a text message in his phone and his call log was empty. I went through his stored numbers and it was only his crew. Damn, I was mad because I couldn't find anything. Maybe he really wasn't cheating. I wondered who was that who called him earlier and why he didn't answer the phone. Smooth moved and I quickly put his phone down and laid down like I was sleeping. He wrapped his arms around me and I thought about all things we have been through. All the promises he made and all the promises that he hasn't broken. Yes he hurt me numerous of times, but I didn't want my family separated. I'm in love with him and I know some women think that I'm foolish for staying with him, but I can't see myself without him. I love him.

Chapter Six

Ebony

Baby Kimora was sitting in her baby rocker watching cartoons on the television. Her eyes were glued to the screen as she watched all the animations and colors. Elmo laughed out loud on the screen and her eyes bucked wider. I laughed as I watched my baby girl. She was three months now and growing up to look just like her father Rich. I missed him and I know he's smiling down on his baby girl. I was busy reading a book called, Sneaky Pussy. So far the book was pretty good. I thought that my story would fit in great with this book by me fucking my best friend since childhood man and having his child. To be honest, at first I felt bad, but after being with him so many times after a while I just didn't give a fuck. I don't regret it and I love our daughter that Rich and I created together. My stomach started growling so I put the book down and went to the kitchen to fix me something to eat. I made me a chicken salad and grabbed a bottled of water out of the fridge. Since last month I lost all of the weight that I gained after having Kimora and I was back down. I stayed consisted with working out and I still had plans on stripping and making me some fast cash. I walked back into the living room and noticed that Kimora had fallen asleep. I turned from Elmo and scanned through the channels and stopped when I noticed that an episode of Love & Hip Hop was on. I watched the stars and fight and keep up drama and thought about how my life would be perfect for reality television. I missed Chicago, but I know that I wasn't able to go back there at all. I had Ant after me for setting him up and there isn't any telling what Shunda had up her sleeve. Fuck them and fuck Chicago. I will just start my life all over in Dallas and raise my baby girl. It was a breath of fresh air to be able to move around and not watch my back. I ate my salad and continued to watch television. I was starting to feel sleepy now, but I didn't want to nap. I got up and took out something for me and Kimora to put on and decided to get dressed and go to the mall. I needed some new clothes to wear and so did Kimora. I still had some money left from the stick ups that Rich was doing. I was watching how I was spending my money and didn't want to run through it. I did all the important things first like paying my bills and stocking the fridge and cabinets. I made sure that Kimora had formula and diapers. I dressed and she woke up crying.

"Don't cry momma's baby. I'm here I know you didn't see your momma," I said as I kissed my sweet Kimora on her tiny forehead.

I went to make her bottle and fed her. After that, I burped her and dressed her. I jumped in my car, but before I pulled off I looked up the directions of the Galleria Dallas mall. I still didn't know my way around Dallas that well yet. With the help of map quest, I made it to the mall. I shopped for Kimora first and then I shopped for me. I bought several dresses and shoes and I also treated myself to a new Louie bag. Once I spent over my limit, it was time for me to go home. Kimora was beginning to get agitated so I headed on home. When we got back, I fed and gave her a bath and put her to sleep. I was so bored so I called my cousin Rio back in Chicago. He answered on the third ring and was happy to hear from me. It was a Monday night so I know that he wasn't really doing too much of nothing.

"What up cuz? It's me Ebony," I said.

"I know what's going on cuz? You good down there in Texas? How is the baby doing?" Rio asked.

"Yes, I'm good just bored as hell. Kimora is doing fine. She's getting bigger too. So what's going on in Chicago?" I said getting straight to the point.

"Same ole bullshit. People getting shot and killed every day. You know me I'm getting my money and staying the fuck out the way," Rio said.

"Have you been going to any parties?" I asked.

"Hell nawl, you know this grinding season. I been hustling and stacking my bread. I just copped me a new whip. I went to go get a new Benz, all white with butter cream seats. I'm going to put some twenty fours on it," Rio said.

"Shit you getting money like that then throw your favorite cousin some cash. I and Kimora could use some," I said.

"Your ass didn't run through all that money yet did you?" Rio asked.

"No, but I'm getting low so throw me some cash. I plan on looking for a job soon though," I said.

"Bet I will buy Kimora something and send the money in the mail with her package tomorrow," Rio said.

"Thank you cuz. Have you heard anything else about Ant again?" I asked.

"Nothing too much, but they still do have a bounty on your head. You know that nigga never really say too much so you better still stay low and always watch your surroundings. If I hear of anything, I will let you know," Rio said.

"Okay cool, I love you and you be safe out there. Goodbye," I said.

"Love you too and I'm sending off everything tomorrow," Rio said before hanging up.

I continued watching another reality television show. I dozed off to sleep on the couch. When I got up my neck had a cramp in it. Kimora was still asleep so I went to go lay down in bed. I was so lonely and in need of some sex. It's been a very long time since I've had some dick. I

69

fantasized about the last sexual experience that Rich and I had. He used to fuck the shit out of me and tell me that my pussy was better than Shunda's pussy. We would have sex three times in a day. One time when I was pregnant while Rich and I was having sex, Shunda called his phone nonstop. Rich finally answered and she was prepared to argue with him. He wasn't trying to hear her bitching so he hung up the phone. She called back and when he answered he put the call on speaker phone so that she can hear us fucking. Shunda heard everything from the moaning to me screaming his name and spelling it. She was pissed, but neither of us cared and continued to fuck. After a while, the silly bitch stopped listening to us and ended the call. I laughed reminiscing about all the times we secretly had sex while she was around and she didn't even know it. I was starting to get horny and began playing with my pussy. I moaned quietly so that I didn't wake Kimora. I opened my legs wider and fingered my pussy until I orgasm. I didn't take any time for me to release. I fell asleep with a smile on my face.

Tuesday was here and I got my lazy ass up and popped in Kenya Moore's workout DVD. I absolutely loved her and her style. During my pregnancy, all I ever watched was reality shows. If I wasn't pregnant during the summer, I wouldn't have been in the house at all. That is how I feel in love with reality television. Being pregnant during the summer is the worst. The only things that I did was eat, watch television, fuck, and sleep. I don't ever want to get pregnant again. Before I began to work out, I checked on Kimora. She was still sleeping, but she needed her diaper changed. While I was changing her diaper, she was smiling and laughing in her sleep. In the back of my mind, I think my father was playing with her. I smiled and went back in the front to work out. I put my hair in a ponytail and stripped down to only my bra and boy shorts. I did every sit up, squat, and push up and forty minutes later I was sweaty and musty.

"Whoa!" I said as I collapsed to the floor for a few minutes to catch my breath.

I was tired, but it was worth it. I dragged my ass to the bathroom to wash the funk off of me. Before I jumped in the shower, I stepped on the scale to weigh myself and noticed that I lost five pounds. Yes all I wanted to do was lose five more and I'll be back down. While I was showering, in the back of mind I was thinking that I needed to start putting my plan to work if I wanted to strip. Today I was going to sign up for pole dancing classes. I also need to hire a babysitter. I want an older lady someone who has experience with babies, who could spend the night if needed, and who really didn't have a life. I know that my mother lives out here and I have her address and number. A part of me wants to call her, but another part of me says fuck her. She ran off into the sunset with another man and never looked back. I need her more than ever since I've become a mom myself. I'm undecided for now, maybe my feelings would change later. Right now, I needed to focus on getting me back together.

Chapter Seven

Tia

"Ladies, today I will be show you how to do pole dancing routines for beginners. Learning how to pole dance for beginners can be a very fun and frustrating process. Don't worry you're in good hands. Today we will start with exercises that will help you develop the flexibility and strength required to do pole dancing."

Hello, I'm Tia Tommy's girlfriend, which is Smooth's cousin that lives in Texas. Please allow me to reintroduce myself. I've been with Tommy since the age of sixteen, seven long years. I come from a big family of women. My mother had five girls and I'm the baby girl. Each one of us are a year apart. Yes my mother had a baby every year. The good thing was that we all had the same father. The bad thing was that he was a deadbeat and really didn't take care of us. My mother had a weak heart and allowed him to come in and out of her life. She always told us that she loves him and would never deny him the opportunity to be a father or spending time with his daughters. Pretty much time is the only thing that he spent on us. Growing up my mother worked her ass off to take care of all five of us. Tamara is the oldest she's twenty six. Traci is second she's twenty five. Trinity the middle sister is twenty four. Tanisha is right before me she's twenty three. Then there is me Tia, I'm the baby girl and I'm twenty two. My mother name is Tabitha and my father name is Timothy. That explains the T's. Growing up with a house full of girls was everything except for calm. When so many personalities clashed, it was chaotic and insane at times. It was moments when we will laugh, cry, and fight, but when it was all over and done with that we all love one another. Each of us possessed a talent. Tamara can sing and play the piano. Traci can do nails. Trinity and I can dance. Tanisha can paint and draw. Our mother invested in all of us and put us in classes. She always said get paid for your talent. She supported us to the fullest and she wanted each one of us to live our life. Death struck our family and last year we lost our father to lung cancer. He was a heavy smoker and by the time we discovered that he was ill unfortunately it was too late. My mother took it extremely hard, but with the help of the five of us we all were there to lift her up when she was down. Overall, my life was pretty decent for a twenty two year old. I grew up fast and like I said I was sixteen when I met Tommy and he was eighteen at the time. I was on my way to school and he was riding down the street in a Buick Regal with some twenty inch rims with his music blasting. At a young age, I was impressed and he caught my attention. Tommy flirted and we exchanged numbers. After that we hooked up and that's when I found out that he was hustling in the streets. Everything was cool; he was getting a little money. Not life changing money, but the type of money that kept me looking nice and I didn't have to ask my mother to pay me much of anything. Two years went by and we were still a couple. During those two years, I had fights over him, he cheated, and I cheated. We were teenagers that were young and crazy in love. I still remained in school, but Tommy didn't and that still didn't stop him and me from going on prom together. We were beautiful and dressed in all white like I was getting married. On the way home from prom the police pulled Tommy over and he was arrested because he had a warrant out on him. When he went to court the next day, he was charged with possession of a firearm. The judge denied him bail and when he was sentenced he gave him twenty four months. I was crushed and I didn't know what to do. Now, it was my turn to hold him down like he held me down. You're about to find out how I started dancing. My older sister Trinity was a stripper, so I linked up with her. I was too young to dance in the clubs, so I only danced at private parties. It was cool and I learned that men loved younger girls. I was cashing out, but I didn't let Tommy know what I was doing. I lied and told him that I was working as an office secretary. My mother and my other sisters weren't aware of me dancing either. I was between Trinity and me until one day one of the private parties that I danced at wasn't so private. Someone had secretly recorded the entire night and the next day it was all over the internet. Everyone found out including my mother and Tommy. My mom was angry and embarrassed. Tommy was pissed and we separated for a month until he realized that he couldn't do that bid by himself. The funny thing about me being exposed was after that I became popular. A lot of men liked my skills and even some of the ladies. I took advantage of that and put them to work. More private parties continued until Tommy was released and he shut that shit down. I had my money saved so I didn't mind and besides I know that he really didn't want to have his girl out there like that. I fell back for a minute, but quickly became bored and opened, Hot Topics, and started teaching pole dancing lessons. When I first started, I only had four students. One year later, I have a day and evening class. I only accept ten students a class and Trinity is my partner. Today, we have nine girls and one boy. Yes I said one boy and you should see him twerk in those heels. I took five and she took five. My group caught on fast and made the hour class a breeze. It seemed like I had quite a few experienced dancers. You see everyone might be able to dance, but they can't pole dance. It isn't hard and as long as you had upper body strength you can achieve it. I loved seeing my students happy after completing my four week sessions. The best part was seeing them doing their tricks on the pole. The hour class was ending soon and I still had to go and the boutique. I wrapped the class up and thanked everyone for coming and told them that I will see them next week.

"Trinity, I'm going by the boutique now. I will see you later for the night class," I said.

"Cool see you later tonight," Trinity said.

The company phone rang and I was about to answer it, but Trinity answered it instead.

"Hot Topics Dance Studio, this is Trinity. How can I help you? Sure we offer weekly classes that you can pay as you go. We also offer four week sessions. Great would you be interested in going during the day or evening?" Trinity asked the customer on the phone.

I smiled and grabbed my Chanel bag and left out the door. I hit the unlock button and jumped in my Audi truck. My phone sang, 'Is it the way you love me baby' by Jill Scott. That was my special ring tone for my boo Tommy. I answered the phone with my sexy voice.

"Hello handsome," I said.

"Hey beautiful. How is your day going so far?" Tommy asked.

"It's going great. How about you? How is your day going?" I asked.

"I'm good just leaving the gym right now. I need you to swing by the house before you go back to the dance studio tonight," Tommy said.

"Ok I will be there by five boo. I love and see you then," I said.

"Love you too shorty," Tommy said.

I drove down the highway wondering what in the hell Tommy wanted to see me for and why it couldn't wait until I got off. Traffic was light and I made it to Hot Topics Boutique without a problem. When I arrived, my sister Tanisha was there assisting a customer. I know you're wondering how I ended up with a boutique. After I met Ciara last year in Chicago and seen Bella Boutique I fell in love. I asked her to help me open my very own and she assisted me. Tommy was happy with the idea and so was my sisters. I pretty much don't have too many friends or hang with a bunch of women. I don't have time for all the drama and worry about the next bitch trying to fuck my man. I don't do gossip unless you talking about money. Real talk that's all I'm talking about. Anyway, I decided to name it the same as my dance studio to sort of build my own brand. Ciara and I thought it was a brilliant idea. On my website you have HotTopics.com you have both of my businesses all you have to do is click on the link of the one that you prefer. It was a few people shopping today so I helped out and assisted the young women. They each bought their items and I thanked them for shopping with me and asked them to come back again.

"Sis is it fine if I leave thirty minutes earlier today? Tommy wants me to stop by the house before I teach my last class tonight," I said.

"It's cool with me. What the hell does he want that it can't wait till you get home tonight?" Tanisha asked.

"Sis I have no idea. You never know with Tommy," I said.

The reminder of the hours flew by. I did all the online orders and prepared them for shipping. Business was great online and was doing numbers. I gathered all the packages and put them inside my truck and drove to UPS to ship. Tommy called my phone and told me that he was waiting on me. It wasn't very crowded so I was in and out. I made it to my house in about twenty minutes. I stay in

Cedar Hill. Tommy and I have a three bedroom home with a two car garage and a pool. I drove into the garage and entered my lovely home. The aroma of vanilla hit my nostrils. I loved the smell of vanilla it always kept me calm. I noticed his MCM luggage at the front entrance. I could hear Tommy in the back room. I switched my sexy ass toward the back where he was. As I walked into the room, Tommy was taking money out of the safe.

"What's up bae? I made it as soon as possible," I said.

"Hey sexy, I need to talk to you. Please don't get upset, but I have to fly to Chicago to handle some business. It's a last minute thing," Tommy said.

"You're not going anywhere without me Tommy," I said as I went to go grab my Louie luggage.

"This is business baby and you can't go," Tommy stopped me and said.

"How long do you plan on being in Chicago?" I asked.

"A week bae and I will be right back," he said as he wrapped his muscular arms around me.

"You promise only a week," I said batted my eyelashes.

"Yes I promise," Tommy said.

He picked me up and carried me to bed. I was small and slim. I was 5'0" brown skinned and I weighed 145lbs. I had a small waist and all my weight went to my ass. Tommy was all man he was 5'7", dark brown and built. He works out and maintains his 185lbs. I tried to speak, but he placed his finger over my mouth. He undressed me then himself. I looked into his eyes as he placed my legs over his shoulders and entered me. He pounded my pussy like it was going to be his last time hitting it. I moaned and begged him to go deeper. Tommy kissed me and said in between moans, "I love your sexy ass."

"I love you too Tommy," I said.

Sweat rolled down the side of his temple and down his chest. He flipped me over and on top of him quickly.

My breast bounced up and down with me like I did on his dick.

"Whose pussy is this?" Tommy asked.

"Yours Tommmmy!" I screamed.

He grabbed my waist and fucked me back until I creamed all over his dick and collapsed on top of him.

Chapter Eight

Ciara

It was time to face my mother Brenda. After shopping around for the children's Halloween costumes and leaving them at home with Smooth, I decided to visit her. I sat in my parked car for a minute to prepare for this moment. It's been two weeks and she has called me nonstop. I made a promise that I'd come by and have a talk with her. Deep down inside why I don't want to face her is because I always said that I would never drink. I thought to myself, 'Never say never.' I got out the car and rang the doorbell. Brenda opened up the door with a smile across her face.

"Ciara come on in baby," she said.

I stepped inside and we both embraced one another. I can hear Kirk Franklin playing in the background. I looked around my mother's apartment and noticed a few new changes. The walls were painted bold mustard and she added more throw pillows to her couch. I smelled something cooking and by the look on my face she read my mind.

"I'm cooking your favorite Beef Neck Bone Soup and Cornbread," she said.

"Really, I see that I came at the right time," I said.

My mother could cook when she wanted to and wasn't drunk and passed out. Beef Neck Bone Soup was my favorite, not only because it was good, but because every time she cooked it Brenda was calmer. I would watch her chop up the onions and throw in the mixed vegetables into the big pot on the stove. I've tried over the years to make it, but it never tasted the way she made it. Brenda went to turn down the music as I sat down. I noticed the bible was opened as if she was reading. She went into the kitchen to check on the food. When she returned back in the living room, she sat down and waited for me to speak. It felt awkward so she spoke first.

"How is everything going? Please don't lie to me because I'm your mother and I can see that something is wrong Ciara. Eric called and told me some things that you were doing. I don't want to hear it from him. I want to hear it from you," Brenda said.

"Well, I've been drinking to ease my mind. You know with everything that has happened within the last year is a lot to handle," I said.

"Yes, it is a lot to handle Ciara, but trust me drinking isn't going to take the pain away. It's only going to make it worse. One minute you start off drinking one glass, then its two glasses. Next thing it's a bottle. You can go from drinking every here and there to drinking to every day," Brenda said.

"When I drink, I don't get drunk like," I paused and stopped talking because I didn't want to hurt her feelings.

"Drunk like me," Brenda finished the sentence.

"Yes, drunk like you mom. I can control it and when I drink it calms me. When you drank in the past, you were the total opposite of calm," I said.

"Child do you think that I started off that way. Ciara it was times that I was so drunk and happy you didn't even know it. As the time went on, the happiness faded and went away. I became a dark and angry person. I took all my anger out on the closet person near me and that was you," Brenda said.

"I've been only drinking wine lately, nothing hard," I said.

"I don't care if you're drinking Pepsi. It's the reason why you're drinking we need to work on in order to get you to stop drinking," Brenda said.

"Starting today, I will stop drinking," I said beginning to get irritated.

"In the meantime, Ciara pray and ask God to help you defeat that illness. He helped me and I know that he could help you. Now, let's go eat some delicious food," Brenda said.

We went in the kitchen and my mother made me a big bowl of her Beef Neck Bone soup with two pieces of cornbread. She even made a pitcher of grape Kool-Aid. That was my favorite and I was surprised that she remembered that. Before we ate, Brenda blessed the food.

"May this food restore our strength, giving new energy to tired limbs, new thoughts to weary minds. May this drink restore our souls, giving new vision to dry spirits, new warmth to cold hearts. And once refreshed, may we give new pleasure to you, who gives us all. Amen," Brenda said.

"Amen," I said.

We sat, ate, and talked for the very first time, just the two of us. For the first time I seen a new woman. Inside I felt like she was transforming into a mother. The feeling was good and her positivity was bouncing off of her and on to me. The food was so good that I got a second bowl and sat back down to continue the conversation. My mother had me laughing as she was telling me about her crazy coworkers and the things that she have seen at her job. We lost track of time and Smooth called me. I could hear the children in the background driving him crazy. I told him that I would be home shortly.

"That was Smooth calling, let me get up out of here. It sounded like the children were giving him a hard time in the background. Thank you for the food," I said.

"Anything for you. Give me a hug before you leave and don't forget what we talked about Ciara," Brenda said.

"No more drinking. I will be back to visit you next week. I love you," I said as I gave her a hug and a kiss.

"Next time bring my grandchildren with you," Brenda said.

I left her house and jumped in the car. I hit the highway and made it home just in time to a house of two sleeping children. Smooth was talking on the phone with someone. I was happy that he put them to bed. Hell, I needed a break sometimes too. I kicked off my shoes and walked over to Smooth who was sitting down in the chair. I massaged his shoulders and kissed the side of his neck as he talked on the phone. I was trying to ear hustle and listen to his conversation. It sounded like he was talking to a man on the phone so I backed up off of him and sat on his lap. Smooth ended the phone call and kissed me on the lips.

"Did you have fun hanging out with your mom?" Smooth asked.

"Yes, I enjoyed myself. Did you have fun hanging out with the kids?" I asked.

"Man those two tried to drive me crazy today. I don't know where they get all that energy from. I was happy when they finally went to sleep," Smooth said.

"All you had to do was put on both of the Despicable Me movies and you wouldn't hear a sound from them," I said laughing.

"Well, I know next time, but let me get out of here. Tommy just got in town so I'm going to meet up with him and the fellas. Wait up for me and have my pussy ready when I get home," Smooth said.

"Tommy is here in Chicago? Did Tia come as well?" I asked.

"Nawl baby, Tia didn't come," Smooth said while lifting me off of his lap.

"Okay well don't be out all night or you going to find your shit on the front lawn," I said.

"Baby quit talking crazy. I will be in at a decent time," Smooth said while kissing me on the lips.

He left out of the door and I went upstairs to my bedroom. I hopped in and out of the shower and grabbed my phone as I sat on my bed. I had to call Tia and find out why Tommy was here without her. I wish Smooth would go out of town without me. Business or no business. I'm surprised Tia even allowed that. Her phone rang and she answered on the first ring.

"Hey Tia, what's going on girl? Smooth told me that Tommy was in town and when I asked did you come he said no," I said.

"Ciara yes and I'm pissed because he just hit me with that bullshit twenty minutes before he left. He called me earlier this morning and asked me to come home before my evening class. Girl, I came home and I see luggage at the door and the first thing that I'm thinking is that he surprised me with a trip," Tia said.

I started laughing, "I'm sorry Tia. I'm not laughing at you; I'm laughing with you. I know you was like where we going bae?" I said.

"Hell yeah, I was going to go pack my luggage and everything. He wouldn't let me saying it was business and that I couldn't come. He gotta be crazy if he thinks I'm going to let him be in another city without me for a week," Tia said.

"Girl a week, hell no that's too long," I said.

"Don't worry I cleared my schedule and I will be flying in on Wednesday," Tia said.

"Girl, I know that shit right. I miss you girl and I can't wait till you get here," I said.

"I miss you too and plus I have to see the new location of your boutique," Tia said.

We talked a few more minutes on the phone before I ended the call. I didn't want to start no bullshit between Tia and Tommy, but I agree with my girl on this one. She should be her hanging out with me. Tommy know he didn't have to worry about her as long as I'm here. That had me thinking overtime in my head if he had another bitch here in Chicago. You never know with these men. I don't put shit past them. I called Kelly and she answered.

"What's up girl?" Kelly said.

"Girl, nothing in the house bored. Where Ant did he go out with Smooth?" I asked.

"Ant said they all had to meet up or some bullshit. Why you ask? Is it something that I need to know?" Kelly asked getting pumped.

"No everything is cool. You know Tommy is in town," I said.

"Really, is Tia here too?" Kelly asked.

"Girl no, and she's pissed too," I said.

"She better be. Her man here in a city filled with thots. I will be pissed too and happily fly my ass right up here," Kelly said.

"She said she's coming Wednesday and don't care what Tommy has to say," I said.

We both started laughing at Tia crazy ass. Kelly and I talked for about forty minutes until her brother Shawn called. I told her to tell him I said hello before I got off the phone with her. I logged on the internet to review my sales and to post my latest items on social media. Three hours had past and I was trying my best to stay up and wait for Smooth. A part of me wanted to call him, but I didn't want to disturb him while he was out taking care of business. Kelly told me not to worry and let him handle his business. I guess she was right so I didn't call. My phone vibrated and rang and I looked down and noticed that it was Smooth sending me a text message. It said, "I love you baby and I will be home in a minute." I smiled as I read it and suddenly all my worries went away. I texted him back and said, "I love you too and I will be waiting for you."

Chapter Nine

Cherish

I sat in my cell reading my letter that I received from my man Lorenzo. I smiled as I reminisced the moments that we shared and how I can't wait to be in his arms again. I miss my man and partner in crime. Yes you heard me say my partner in crime. He was the one who introduced me to scamming. I met him through my coworker who later on became my best friend Mya. Mya and Lorenzo are cousins. She introduced us to one another one day at her barbecue. From there we dated and it was great that eventually we started a relationship. I know you're thinking I'm just a girl from the hood with a crack head mother and a gang of sisters and brothers. If you are, then you're wrong. I'm actually a girl that was raised is Richton Park with both of my parents in the home. My mother is a stay at home mom. She met my father in college and they have been together since then. My father is a fireman. He provided for the family. I'm the only child and I it wasn't anything that I ask for that I didn't get. It's funny that I'm sitting in MCC Chicago for check fraud. Things changed when my father was killed in a fire. My mother took hard, but two months later she started dating one of my father's friends. Crazy as hell, that meant that the both of them had been fucking around. My mother allowed him to move into our home. A month later is when he be ginned to molest me. Of course, I told my mother, but she didn't believe me. He would do it when my mom went somewhere and sometimes he would come into my bedroom at night. My mother caught him and she still blamed me. Me being a child and not knowing any better I blamed myself as well. I took full responsibility for my actions. Besides he didn't put a gun to my head and force me to do anything. My mother had hopes and dreams of me going to college and meeting a successful man who could take care of me. Just like repeating history and my mother felt that if it worked for her then it could work for me. When I turned eighteen, I rebelled and did whatever the hell I wanted to do. My mother couldn't control and her boyfriend didn't stop me because he was afraid that I will tell on him. I started dating boys. Some were corny as hell and some were down to earth just like me and smoked, drank, and partied. Just because I lived in Richton Park, it didn't stop me from having fun. When the parents were away, the children will play. I'm talking house parties with all the drugs and alcohol you could have. Of course, there was sex involved and lots of it. I wasn't a promiscuous girl, but I did have sex with few boys here and there. When I finished high school, I left home. I didn't go away to college. I moved out and got my own place with the money that I saved for a year. I moved to Country Club Hills and got a job at South Suburban Hospital working in medical records. That's where I met Mya who was my coworker at the time. She always came to work rocking designer labels and she pushed a cute Acura. There was only two ways where I imagined that a twenty year old got the cash from because our little eleven dollars hour job was doing it. She either came from money or had a man with money. I linked up with her quickly because I wanted the same type of life. While we were hanging out from time to time, I noticed that she didn't come from a family with money or had a man with money either. I wondered where the money came from and one day when we went shopping I found out from where. We were at Oak Brook Mall and went to Victoria Secret, Neiman Marcus, Apple, and Burberry. She swiped card after card and every transaction went through. I didn't know how she was paying for it, but she let me get a few things so I wanted to know where all the money she spent came from. When we're sitting down eating, she explained to me that she has gifts cards and that she steals other people money from their checking accounts or apply for cards in people names. I asked how she did it and how can I be down. That's when I learned that she takes down the social security numbers from the patient's at the hospital. I didn't care that it was illegal and I wanted to be down and asked her to put me on. Mya called up Lorenzo and told him that I was interested. That's when I met him at the barbecue and business turned to pleasure. He thought I was cute. I mean I am, but at the time I felt like I was basic. A brown skinned skinny girl who weighed 125lbs and was 5'2". The thing that I loved the most was that I wore my natural hair. No perm was needed and sometimes I will rock an afro or sometimes I would get it professionally straighten. When I start getting money, my lifestyle changed but I didn't get to out of hand with it. Eventually, Mya got caught and was fired. I didn't stay to much longer because I knew that they were watching the employees so after a while I resigned. When I left my job, I had close to three hundred patient's social security numbers, from there the money started pouring in. My mother noticed the change in my lifestyle and she thought I was selling pussy. I remember the day when my mother sat me down and asked me if I was an escort. I laughed and told her that I was a bill collector and received bonuses on occasions. She believed it until I was arrested in a True Religion store for swiping a card that wasn't mine. I went to court and was charged with credit card fraud and by it being my first time I received twelve months' probation. Lorenzo was there for me throughout everything. Our relationship grew and he and I eventually lived together. Lorenzo bought a house in Orland Park from all that money that he was profiting from. Life was pretty good and I didn't have a care in the world. That was until I started to get to greedy and didn't want to listen to Lorenzo and make moves without him. I recruited my own little team of girls and that was an epic fail. That's why I'm sitting in here now. I'm just happy that Lorenzo hasn't turned his back on me and his unborn child. He was happy that I was pregnant. He better be lucky that I'm locked up or else I would've been at the chop shop like I did the other two. I was only twenty one years old and I didn't plan on having any children not until I was in my late twenties. Well shit happens and you could either step in it or step over it. I choose to accept my baby that's growing inside me. I was afraid to have my baby alone and to go through this pregnancy by myself. With the help of Kayla, she made my time here a little better. We clicked in a major way and we both had one another's back. I continued to read my letter and Kayla walked in to check on me.

"Hey Cherish. Oh I see you got some mail from your love bug," Kayla said.

I put my letter away. "Yes my man make sure that he writes me every week," I said.

"That's cool, but I'm about to go and make a phone call," Kayla said.

"I might as well walk with you to the phones and make a phone call myself," I said.

We walked to the phones and I called Lorenzo. He answered the phone on the first ring.

"Hello, hey baby, what's up?" Lorenzo said.

"You are Mr. I just received your letter today. It put a smile on my face. What are you doing? Can you talk at the moment?" I said

"Just doing a little shopping, but I always have time to talk to you. I was hoping that it made you smile. How are you doing? How is my baby doing inside your belly?" Lorenzo said.

"She's doing fine. I think I found a name for our daughter," I said.

"Really, what would you like to name our daughter?" Lorenzo asked.

"Laniyah is what I would like to name our daughter," I said.

"Laniyah is a pretty name. I like it," Lorenzo said.

"I knew that you would. Well, I don't want to hold you up. I will just call you back tonight around eight p.m. I miss you and I love," I said.

"I love you too Cherish. One," Lorenzo said.

I laughed because Lorenzo was always saying one instead of goodbye. I looked over to Kayla to see if she was ready to go back, but she was yelling at someone on the phone. She noticed that I was ready, but she waved me on indicating that it was cool if I went on ahead. Kayla was pissed off at whoever she was talking to. It sounded like it was her baby daddy that she was cursing out. I'm so happy that Lorenzo and I don't do all that. I'm really not a confrontational type of person. A lot of people thought because I was small that I was soft and innocent. They didn't have a clue and I liked it that way.

Kayla

I had to call Smooth to talk to him. I missed hearing his voice and we have been only connecting through Coorlinks. He said that he's been busy and haven't forgotten about me. Every time I call him he sends me to voicemail. I try to call him when I know that Ciara isn't around. Or I hit him up when I know that he is out and about. On my way to the phones, I stopped to check on Cherish and she walked to make a phone call as well.

Sitting in front of the phone, I decided to call Aaliyah instead and then I would have her call Smooth. I don't have time to be playing games that nigga was going to talk to me. I quickly dialed her number and she picked up. All I heard was children playing in the background. The automated voice spoke informing her that someone from a federal institution was calling.

"Hey, what's up Kayla?" Aaliyah said.

"Hey have you seen Smooth lately? Every time I call his phone that nigga don't pick up," I said.

"Yes, he was by here last night with Vell. Is everything okay?" Aaliyah asked?

"Hell nawl! Click over and call him for me," I said.

Aaliyah clicked over and called Smooth. He answered the phone with music blasting in the background.

"Hello what the fuck is up Smooth? Why are you avoiding me?" I yelled.

Smooth turned the music down, "Kayla ain't anybody avoiding your ass. I've been busy," Smooth said.

103

"Busy my ass! You too damn busy to answer your damn phone for your baby momma?" I said.

"Aye, you better lower your tone. I don't know who the fuck you think you're talking to," Smooth said.

I exhaled and calmed down. I didn't want him to hang up on me. It's already been a week since I've last heard from him. So I lowered my voice.

"I feel like I'm chasing you down and sweating you. I'm in here pregnant and all emotional and shit. When I call and you don't answer I feel like you're on some fuck Kayla type shit," I said.

"You know what I'm sorry. How are you doing Kayla?" Smooth asked.

"I'm doing better now that I've heard from you," I said.

"That's cool, but when I hit you back online I told you that I was busy. I don't want you to ever think that it's fuck Kayla. Do you understand?" Smooth said.

"Yes, I do understand. I need for you to understand that we need to talk more often. It's been a week too long and I'm just not some random chick. So when I call you need to answer," I said.

"No problem, let me get off this phone. I'm out here handling some business. Can you call me back tonight?" Smooth said.

"Yes I will just answer your phone," I said with an attitude.

"Bet ok," Smooth said and hung up the phone.

I could still here the noise in the background from Aaliyah's house. So that meant she was still on the line.

"Aaliyah, are you still there?" I asked

She didn't respond. Damn, she put the phone down.

"Aaliyah!!!" I yelled for the second time.

"Hello. Are you two finished talking? I'm sorry I put the phone down. I didn't want to hear your conversation," Aaliyah said.

"It's cool. What the hell are you doing anyway?" I asked.

"I'm trying to comb my daughter hair. Are you cool now since you have talked Smooth?" Aaliyah said.

"Yes I feel better now. I just had to check his ass that's all," I said.

"Well don't let him get to you. Kayla remember that you are pregnant and how you act and respond to things affects your baby. If you yell and cry, your baby is going to the same thing. I don't want a yelling and crybaby ass god daughter," Aaliyah said.

"You're right about that, but girl sometimes he takes me there," I said.

"I totally understand that. Vell made me snap off earlier. So I know how you feel just relax and stay calm. Think about positive things. I want a healthy god baby," Aaliyah said.

"What did Vell do Aaliyah?" I asked.

"I will tell you later. The children around and I don't like to talk in front of them," Aaliyah said.

"Okay well, I'm sleepy and about to take a nap. Thanks for calling him and for the advice. I will call you back tomorrow," I said.

"Alright talk to you later chick," Aaliyah said.

Chapter Ten

Aaliyah

Once I got off the phone with Kayla, I continued to comb my daughter hair. I had one more to go. I shook my head as I parted her hair. They had so much hair on their heads thanks to me and Vell. I'm Aaliyah, Vell's girl. He and I have been rocking for five years now. It's funny how we both met. I was riding down Central Avenue and as soon as I drove out into the intersection and was about to pass up Chicago Avenue out of nowhere a white Jeep jumps in front of me. I punched down on my brakes. Screech! I'm happy that I had some good brakes. The Jeep kept on rolling. Me being me I followed that mutherfucker. I was pissed and on ten. I have a severe case of road rage and I was ready to curse that nigga out. He seen me and sped up weaving through traffic. I stayed on his ass and several cars noticed that I was chasing him and they got out of the way. He made a right on Augusta Avenue and was hitting it. I caught up with him when he got caught at the right light on Laramie.

"Nigga, you driving like you're the only person out here on the road. What the fuck is wrong with you jumping out in front of me? I should get out this car and fuck you up!" I yelled.

"My fault shorty. I see you and I wasn't going to hit you. I'm sorry," he said.

"Whatever, you need to wait your turn like everybody fucking else," I said.

He was high as hell and the car smelled like weed. I turned my nose up. The cars behind us began to blow their horns because the light turned green. I rolled my eyes and he pulled off and sped down the street. I continued to go home and once I made it my friend Kia called me. I told her about the incident and she thought I was crazy for following him. She changed the subject and asked me to come and hang out with her tonight at a kickback. I told her that I would try to make it and she said that was fine. I cleaned up my place and took a cat nap once I was done. Later on that night, I got dressed and ready to go to a kickback that my friend Kia invited me to. A kickback is a gathering that is usually thrown at a hotel. Everyone just chill, smoke, drink, mingle and kickback. When I got there, I was impressed because whoever was throwing it had reserved a suite. I walked passed a few people that I know and said hello and asked if they had seen Kia. They pointed toward the back and there is where I found her.

"Hey Aaliyah, what's up? I'm so happy that you came. This is nice ain't it girl?" Kia said.

"Yes it's cool," I said trying to act like I wasn't impressed.

"Let's go and get something to drink. The bar is over there," Kia said.

We walked over to the bar that they had set up. They had all the liquor you can drink. Patron, Ciroc, Goose, Hennessy, 1738, Wine. Shit they had everything. The girl asked us what we wanted to drink. Kia and I both got a cup of Ciroc and lime. We tipped the girl and walked back over to the wall.

"Who is throwing this kickback?" I asked.

"This guy named Red I know and his friends," Kia said.

"It's nice and not ratchet," I said.

"Red and his people don't throw ratchet shit. I told you that you would like it," Kia said.

The music played and we mingle and talked to a few people that we knew. A few boys tried to talk to me, but I didn't come there to meet anyone. I only came to chill. I walked over to the bar to get another drink. I ask for another cup of Patron. The girl told someone to tell a person by the name of Vell that they were out of Patron.

"Give me a few minutes. They're about to bring out so more Patron," the girl said.

"Okay cool," I said.

I stepped back so that she could serve the rest of the people. I looked over at Kia and she was running her mouth talking to some tall boy. A moment later a boy walked over carrying a case of Patron. He sat the box down and took out several bottles and opened them for the girl who was serving the drinks. When he looked up, I noticed his face and realized that he was the boy that I cursed out earlier on Augusta and Laramie. The girl asked him to pour me a cup of Patron. He looked up and noticed that it was me. I rolled my eyes.

"That's okay I don't want anything to drink," I said and walked away.

As I walked off he said, "Hey mean girl."

I walked back over to Kia and the boy who she was talking to and told her that I was leaving.

"Bye Kia I'm leaving," I said with an attitude.

"Why are you leaving? What's wrong?" Kia asked.

"Remember the boy who I told you about and cursed out earlier," I said.

"Yes, I remember. What about him?" Kia asked.

"He's here so I'm leaving," I said.

Vell walked over to me, Kia, and the tall boy who Kia was talking to. The two of them exchanged words.

"What's up mean girl? Kia is this your friend?" Vell asked.

Kia starting laughing, but I didn't think shit was funny. "Yes, this is my friend Aaliyah. Aaliyah this is Red and this is his friend Vell," Kia introduced the both of them.

"What's going on?" Red asked confused.

"Nothing, I was preparing to leave. Kia, I will call you when I make it home," I said walking off.

As I turned to leave, someone grabbed my arm. I turned around and seen that it was the boy Vell.

"Please don't go allow me to reintroduce myself. I'm Vell," he said reaching out to shake my hand. I smacked his hand away. Kia looked at me and rolled her eyes. Red laughed.

"Damn Aaliyah, stop being so extra. You're so damn stubborn," Kia said.

"Aaliyah, I apologize about earlier today. Can you put that behind us and stay to enjoy the rest of the kickback?" Vell said.

I rolled my eyes and flipped my hair. "Okay and Kia I'm not being extra or stubborn. I'm…." Before I could finish my sentence, Vell cut me off.

"You're beautiful," Vell said.

I tried not to smile, but when Kia and Red started laughing so did I. Vell starting laughing as well so I decided to cool off and to stop acting like a bitch. Kia was right sometimes I could be stubborn at times. For the rest of the night Vell and I engaged in a deep conversation and exchanged numbers. The next following weekend we went out on our date to Lucky Strikes and had a good time. Three years and a set of twins later we are still together. It hasn't been the best we have had our share of good times and bad ones. When I mentioned that he made me snap earlier, it was because he was being nice with our next door neighbor. Vell and I stay in Berkeley in a three bedroom townhome. Our neighbor is a single black female. I'm not going to hate she's attractive and has a great shape. Earlier today when I stepped out on the porch her and Vell were talking and laughing. I politely walked over and introduced myself. She was pleasant, but I didn't like that shit. I could tell by the look in her eyes that she wants my man. Vell was just standing there looking with a smile on his face that I wanted to smack off. So when Vell and I got inside the house I told him I bet not catch him in her face again. He said I was over reacting. I don't think so and I'm going to be watching Miss Thang for now on. I know she sees everything. From the cars Vell and I drive and from the way we carry ourselves. I don't even know much about her, but my goal is to find out who she is and where she's from. Anyway enough about Miss Thang and back to me, I love Vell and our family. Do I trust Vell? Hell no, simply because I see how Smooth has a woman at home and also has another woman in jail carrying his child. Do you blame me for thinking that my man could be on the same thing? Although Vell says that he isn't on that, but let's be honest, if my best friend did hoeish things my man would think that I did the same. That's one of the reasons why Kia and I are no longer friends because supposedly she fucked Red and Ant. Vell says he didn't fuck her, but I believe he fucked her too. You just never know with Kia, every guy was her friend or play brother. I can't wait till Kayla has her baby and gets out of jail. It's going down baby and I'm going to make sure that I have the best seat in the house. Don't get it twisted, Kayla is my girl and we have grown to be cool. Kayla says that she's not keeping her baby a secret or hiding her baby from Ciara. I don't fuck with Ciara, but I do feel sorry for her. I mean she just accepted another child and next year she will be hit with another one. Smooth ain't shit, but then again that ain't my business. My business is Vell and to make sure he doesn't pull that stunt on me. I'm not like Ciara. I will kill him, that bitch, and the baby too.

Smooth

Kayla almost made me say fuck her and that baby. I know that I haven't talked to her lately, but shit I been getting money. My cousin Tommy was in town and now it was time to handle business. I understand that she's doing time for me, but I also make sure that she is straight inside there. I had too much other bullshit going on right now at the moment. Ciara and I have to do counseling because I got my girl drinking and shit. I don't feel good about what I have put her through. That's why I thinking about moving Kayla and the baby down in Texas to keep her away from

116

Ciara. I would be doing a lot of traveling down there and that would be the perfect time to spend with her and my child. I love Ciara and if she finds out about this child it would kill her. I didn't try to get Kayla pregnant and if she wasn't locked up I would've sent her to the chop shop. She's a different type of crazy. You know the type of crazy that wants attention. By her being locked up and not being able to see me is driving her crazy. So when she gets out she's going to want all my attention. The problem is I can't do that and it's not going to easy. Ciara comes first before any woman and I know the moment when Kayla fell that I'm neglecting her she's going to act crazy. The last thing I wanted to do was put my hands on Kayla like I did in the past. She was carrying my child now so I wanted to treat her as such. Luckily, I still had six months to decide what I was going to do. In the meantime, I was focusing on getting Ciara the help that she needs. I still had plans on marrying her. I also want another child with her then after that no more. I was getting money and at the rate I was going I planned on making more. At times, I have the devil in one ear and god in the other ear. I had a lot on my mind and I really needed to talk to someone other than my boys. I picked up my phone and called the one lady that I loved the most. I asked her if it was fine if I came by and she told me yes.

My mother answered the door and greeted me with a big hug and kiss.

"Hey son, how are you doing?" my mother asked.

"I'm doing fine just stopping by to check on you," I said.

She gave me a look, "You know I'm doing fine. How's my grandchildren and Ciara?" she asked.

"They're doing fine," I said with my head hanging low. I quickly changed the subject and asked, "Are you frying catfish?"

"I just finished frying some. It's in the kitchen. Help yourself to a plate," my mother said.

I went in the bathroom to wash my hands. After that I went in the kitchen and grabbed me a plate. I loved my mother cooking. I see she also fried some green tomatoes. I made myself a plate, grabbed the hot sauce, and a Pepsi.

When I got back in the dining room my mother still had the look on her face.

"What? Why are you looking at me like that?" I asked laughing.

"You're my son and I know you like the back of my hand. I can tell when something is going on. You didn't come by here to check on me and eat my food. You can't fool me," my mother said.

I chewed on the piece of catfish before I could respond. My mother's piercing eyes remained on me until I opened my mouth and said, "Kayla is pregnant and it's my child."

My mother got up and smacked me across my head.

"Ouch! What you do that for Ma?" I said rubbing my head.

"Fool is you crazy? You just pull the same bullshit with the other girl, Rochelle, and you see how that ended. What is wrong with you? Does Ciara know?" my mother asked.

"No, she doesn't and I don't think that I could tell her," I said.

"What the hell you mean? You don't think you could tell her? You can't keep a baby hid away. How many months is she?" my mother asked.

"Three months she has the baby in April," I said.

"That poor girl is having a baby while she's locked up. Eric I just can't believe what I'm hearing right now. Ciara is going to kill you and this time I'm not bailing you out of this one. Ain't any need to be looking all pitiful and shit now. What's done is done," my mother said while shaking her head.

I looked pitiful. I know I was wrong, but I honestly didn't know what to do. I was hoping that my mother had my back.

"I just can't tell Ciara now. Ma she's drinking and that's a problem that we already have to deal with," I said.

"Lord Jesus take the wheel. She's doing what? Does her mother know? After she finds out about this she's going to do more than drinking. Eric what has gotten into you? I didn't raise you like this. It's bad enough that I already accept the fact that you're in the streets, but I'm not accepting you having babies here, there, and everywhere. You need to get your act together," my mother said.

"I know I messed up. Her mother knows about her drinking problem. Ciara and I are starting counseling soon. Ma, I just want everything back the way it used to be," I said.

My mother remained quiet and just shook her head. She was mad and disgusted with me. Like she said, it was bad enough that I was a hustler. I know that I did my wrong doings and ain't no need to hide them. I just have to be a man and put everything out on the table.

Chapter Eleven

Halloween

Tia

My bags were packed and I was ready to catch my fight to Chicago. I made sure that my sisters were in charge with dancing studio and boutique. There was no way that I was allowing Tommy to be away from me in another city, not me baby. I called him and told him that I booked my fight and that I was looking forward to seeing him once I got there. He said cool and that was all. Tommy knew better. I called Ciara to inform her that I will be there and she and Kelly can't wait to see me. I needed a break anyhow. I usually only get a chance to take a trip during the summer so it felt good to get away during the fall. I took a cab to the airport and boarded my flight. Once the plane was in the friendly skies, I closed my eyes and fell asleep.

Two hours later I arrived in Chicago. I went to Avis to pick up my rental car. I didn't call Tommy to tell him that I made it. I wanted to pop up on his ass. I put in the address to the Westin Hotel where Tommy was staying. I was so excited to be in Chicago so that I could spend time with my girls. I loved my sisters and all, but it was time to chill with my friends. I called Ciara up and she was just starting the children's Halloween party. I told her that I would swing by her house after I changed my clothes. I arrived at the hotel in thirty minutes. I went to the clerk at the front desk where Tommy said that he would have the extra key. Room 122 was where I was headed. I placed the card in the door. Once I stepped inside, I noticed that the room was clean. Tommy had a few clothes across the bed. I placed my purse down on the table. "Tommy," I said, but he didn't answer. I heard a noise coming from the back. I walked toward the back and I heard the noise even clearer. I know I wasn't hearing what I thought I was hearing. I heard moans. Oh hell nawl! I said to myself while I took my earrings off and put my hair in a ponytail. I know Tommy not fucking another bitch in here. I stormed in the back where the Jacuzzi and no one were there. I looked over at the wall and it was a porno playing on the television.

"Looking for me?" Tommy said.

I jumped from the sound of Tommy's voice. I turned around and hit him on the chest.

"You scared the shit out of me," I said while holding my chest.

"I just came back from the gym," Tommy laughed and took off his sweaty tank top.

"I thought you were back her fucking some bitch. I was ready to kick you and that bitch ass, but when I got back here it was a porno playing," I said.

"Why would I have another female in my room when I was expecting you? That's some silly shit," Tommy said.

"You better not have a female in her period rather you expecting me or not," I said.

"Tia, please stop tripping baby. You're in Chicago with me. Let's not argue," Tommy said.

I didn't say anything else. Tommy was right I was here in Chicago and it was time to turn up. I unpacked my things. I joined him in the bathroom and pulled the shower curtain back. Tommy looked at my naked body. I had a mischievous grin on my face and he stepped to the side to let me in.

"I'm so sorry baby for not trusting you and always accusing you of cheating on me," I said.

"I love you and only you and only you Tia," Tommy said.

He pinned me up against the shower wall and his dick went inside me. I moaned softly and grabbed on to him with my legs wrapped around his waist. The water hit Tommy's back and some of it hit me across the face. "Ohhhh yes Tommy! I miss you so much!" I said as he plunged in me.

"I miss you too bae," Tommy said.

He went deeper and deeper inside me. I dug my nails in his back and begged him to speed it up. He took me by the waist and guided my hips. I kissed his muscled arms, chest, and finally his lips.

"Tia, I love this pussy. Whose pussy is this?" Tommy said.

"Your pussy Tommy!" I moaned.

"Spell it," Tommy said.

"T O M M Y," I said spelling out his name.

Ding Dong! I heard someone come to the door. She opened the door and hugged me.

"Hey Tia girl! Come on in!" Kelly said.

"Hey Kelly boo. What's going on? How have you been?" I asked.

"Girl, I've been doing fine. Going to school and focusing on getting my degree in Real Estate. Ciara and the kids are in the basement where the Halloween party is just follow me," Kelly said.

I followed Kelly downstairs where Ciara and a basement of screaming kids were. The music was playing. There was pizza, wings, chips, and candy. The decorations were spooky, but in a fun type of way. The children were in their costumes playing and dancing. I spotted Ciara in the corner taking pictures of a group of children. Kelly and I walked over to where she was and Kelly told her to turn around. Ciara seen me and screamed.

"Tia girl look at you. You look so nice and you glowing girl," Ciara said hugging me.

"Thank you and so are you," I said hugging my friend back.

Ciara introduced me to a few more parents of the children. Everyone was so nice and friendly. I was so surprised because I heard a lot of bad things about Chicago and the people that live there. Ciara, Kelly, and I sat down and we ate.

"Girl this chicken is good. Where did this come from?" I asked eating my chicken wing.

"A chicken place named Uncle Remus," Ciara and Kelly laughed.

"Ya'll going to have me fat. Hand me a slice of pizza too," I laughed.

"Girl you have to teach us how to get up and down on that pole," Kelly said.

127

"Anytime whenever you are ready. It's pretty easy and you will do great," I said.

"What did Tommy say when he first seen you?" Ciara asked.

"Girl it's more like what did he do," I laughed.

We all started laughing. Some of the kids stopped and looked at us.

"Ciara this party is all that. I tip my hat off to you. You should receive the Mommy of the year award," I said.

"Thank you. I just want to give my children the life that I didn't have when I was a child. I've never experienced this and I promised that one day when I become a mom my child would never go through what I had to go through," Ciara said.

I sat back and imagined how I would be as a mom. I know Tommy and I would be great parents. I always wanted two kids, a house, with a dog. I know it sounds corny, but sometimes I like corny. We sat back, talked, and enjoyed the rest of the party. The children had a great time and so much fun. It was eight p.m. and I left to go back to the hotel to prepare for the night. Tommy called me and told me that he would be waiting on me. Ciara walked me to the door. I was about to ask about Smooth and he came walking through the door.

"Hey Tia," Smooth said while giving me hug.

"Hey Smooth. How's everything?" I asked. Ciara stood back and smiled.

"Cool. My cousin waiting for you at the hotel. I just left that nigga," Smooth said.

"I'm on my way back there now. Ciara, I will call you girl once I'm ready," I said.

"Where ya'll going?" Smooth asked laughing looking back and forth at Ciara and me.

"We going to the Sawtooth, that's where we going," Ciara said pointing at me and her.

Smooth grabbed Ciara playfully and started kissing her and telling her that she wasn't going anywhere tonight. I laughed and told Ciara goodbye and walked out the door and left the two love birds alone.

Ciara

I gathered up all my girls for a ladies night out. We all met up at the Sawtooth and I had a section waiting for us. It was Me, Kelly, Tia, London, and I invited Denise. Me and Kelly was there waiting for the other ladies to arrive. I said hello and made small talk to a few familiar faces. I was looking good wearing a black lace dress that showed off my thick thighs and a black pair of four inch heels. My jet black Peruvian hair dropped down to my ass with a wavy texture. Kelly rocked a brown bouncy bob. She had on an opened back jumpsuit that exposed her tattoo on the lower part of her back. The heels she had on gave her height. She received a lot of compliments. I loved it when all the women asked where she got her jumpsuit from and she would tell them from Bella Boutique. That was a hot piece that I got in the other day and I knew Kelly would be the perfect person to pull it off. We sat down and Tia walked in wearing a nude tank dress and some nude red bottoms. Her dress was painted on her. The gold accessories were perfect. Tia turned heads with her round derriere. We waved for her to come over. Shortly after Denise and London arrived looking beautiful. Denise had on a red and white bandage dress that hugged her body. Her booty popped out and so did her bouncy curls. She switched over in her red heels and joined us. London had on a brown mini dress that matched her brown eyes. Her brown thigh boots was to die for. She said to a few people as she walked over to join us. I was so happy to be out and away from kids.

"I'm so glad that everyone made it. Tia this is London my assistant and this is Denise, Red's girlfriend," I said introducing everyone.

"Hello and finally nice to meet you London. Nice to meet you as well Denise," Tia said.

"Nice to meet you too Tia," Both London and Denise said.

Kelly talked to the bartender who walked over to us and placed our orders as the rest of us sat back and talked. London and Tia talked amongst themselves, while I, Kelly, and Denise discussed our men. The bottles of Ciroc arrived at our table. Everyone poured their drinks. Kelly poured mine only filling my glass halfway and adding more juice for the other half. I quickly gulped down my glass and reached for the bottle to refill mine up. Kelly slightly pushed my hand away and poured me a glass of juice instead. The other girls didn't notice what she was doing. I signaled for the bartender and asked for a of bottle water. I could see that I wasn't going to win this fight with Kelly. The bartender came back and gave me my water. Kelly gave me a look of approval. I enjoyed the rest of the night and didn't worry about not drinking because I had a bottle of Riesling waiting for me at home in my secret hiding place.

We left the club and I made it home by two a.m. Smooth and I texted all night and I knew that he was still out as well. The children were at my mom's place. I rushed over to my hiding place where I kept the cleaning supplies and grabbed the bottle of Riesling. Smooth would never think twice about looking there. That nigga didn't clean up. I poured me a glass and placed it back behind the Pine-Sol. 'Only one glass is all I need,' I said to myself in my head. The wine made me so mellow and horny. It calmed me and immediately I called Smooth.

"Where you at Daddy? Hurry up home; I can't wait to suck your big dick," I said seductively on the phone.

"Damn babe, you got my dick hard. Daddy will be home soon and ready to stick this dick down your throat," Smooth said.

"I will be waiting," I said.

I went to shower and once I got out I oiled my dark skinned. After that, I put on my sexy lingerie and a masquerade mask that was purple. I sprayed Romance on my body and looked to admire myself in the mirror. All I was missing was some lipstick. I applied my purple shade of Mac lip gloss and blew a kiss at myself in the mirror. I heard the alarm say, "Front door opened." I quickly laid across the bed on my side with my ass poked out with my left hand placed behind my head. Smooth entered the room and was shocked to see me like that. He smiled and rubbed his dick. I smiled and seductively said, "Trick or Treat."

Chapter Twelve

Ebony

Time was going by fast and Kimora was growing. It was November and I have grown to love Dallas. It was certainly different right now this time year, the weather and even the people during the holiday season. If I was in Chicago right now, it would be cold and people would be running around crazy preparing for the holiday. Thanksgiving was right around the corner. I'm so glad I had a change of scenery. I hired a baby sitter her name is Stella. Stella was sixty years old and had over twenty years of experience. When I went to get my nails done, I asked the nail tech if she knew any babysitters and she gave me Stella's information. I called her up and luckily she was available to babysit Kimora. Stella told me her rates and offered the first week for free. I said no problem. The first week went great and Kimora felt comfortable with her. Miss Stella gave me that grandma type of feeling. I made myself a list of things I need to do. I have to join a gym really soon and get a gym membership. I wanted to keep my body in tip top shape. The at home exercises served its purpose. Now, it was time to put in work. I signed up for pole dancing lessons. If I was going to be a stripper, I had to do more than dancing. I had to learn how to climb that pole. I enrolled in the six week course at Hot Topics Dancing Studio. The nail tech also said that she was the best. The instructor was young and very experienced. During my first week, I watched her and wondered what her story was. I knew that she was much too young to running a business like this without having a boss nigga in her corner. I even heard that she owned a boutique as well. Where I'm from in Chicago, if you were a young black woman who owned business, drug money was involved. I was going to find out who was her man maybe we could creep off on low. In the meantime, I was focusing on getting myself together and finding a man who can take care of me and Kimora. I went straight home after dance practice and when I walked in Kimora was in her high chair eating smashed up greens and cornbread. I kissed my baby girl on her fat cheeks. She smiled and continued to eat her food. Miss Stella was sitting on the couch watching a Lifetime movie. I sat down next to her.

"Miss Stella what you watching?" I asked.

135

"Child, some movie about this cop breaking into women homes and raping and murdering them," Stella said.

"Sounds good," I said.

"All Lifetime movies are good. I cooked fried chicken, black eye peas with greens and cornbread. Child, I had to go to the grocery store to buy some real food. I don't eat that mess you have in your fridge," Stella said.

I laughed at Miss Stella. She was right all I had was healthy food in my fridge. I had to lose my pounds and eating like the way I did in Chicago will have me big as a house. Don't get me wrong, I love my curves, but you're not really consider thick if your stomach was bigger than you ass. No guts over here. The food smelled good and I was going to enjoy me just a small portion. I love me some cornbread and I can tell that the food was good at the way Kimora was eating.

"Kimora is sure enjoying it. I'm going to help myself to a plate," I said.

"Knock yourself out," Stella said.

I walked in the kitchen and fixed myself a plate. The food was delicious and when I was done I rubbed my belly. I think I could get used to having Stella around. I went back into the living room and Miss Stella was changing Kimora diaper. The movie was gone off and Stella threw away the diaper and went to wash her hands. I picked Kimora up and smothered her with kisses. Miss Stella left and we told her that we would see her tomorrow. She jumped in her Honda Accord and drove off. I turned to the Nick Jr. and put Kimora in her walker. I ran me some bath water and poured my Epsom salt in it to soak. The pole dancing was a workout as well. I soaked in the tub and closed my eyes and wondered what it would be like for me to strip. What would my stripper name be? How much money could I make? My mind was working and I had a lot to think about. When I got out of the tub, Kimora was still in the same place where I left her watching television.

The next day I had a nail appointment. I was going to find out everything from the nail tech about Tia. I had to find out about her and I knew that I wasn't going to get close to her because Tia kept to herself. I walked in on time to get my nails done and sat down in the chair.

"Hey Cassandra girl, how are you today?" I said being phony.

"I'm doing just fine. How are you?" Cassandra asked.

"I'm doing fine just fine," I said sitting down in the chair.

"What are you getting today?" Cassandra asked.

"A no chip manicure and a pedicure," I said.

Cassandra did my pedicure first. I picked out a pretty color called Warm &Toasty Turtleneck. It was in the purple family and it was perfect for the fall and colorful. I let Cassandra concentrate on my toes and once she started on my manicure I started my conversation.

"I started my dancing lessons last week at the place you recommended. The owner Tia she is pretty young to be running a place like. I bet she got herself a really good man who helped her out," I said and I didn't cut any corners. I got straight to the point.

138

"Tia is really cool and talented," Cassandra said trying to dodge my question.

"Wait let me pay you now for my services," I said pulling out my wallet. I paid her for the manicure and pedicure and added an extra fifty. Cassandra counted the money and caught on quickly. She stuffed the money in her bra and started talking.

"Tia is twenty two and she goes with this nigga named Tommy. They have been together since they were teenagers. I believe Tommy is twenty four. Girl, he is fine and has a body like 50 cent. He's paid and rumor has it he's about to take over Dallas and Houston," Cassandra said.

"I knew Tia was fucking with a hustler. How could I get close to him? Where does he hang out at?" I asked Cassandra.

"Now, that I don't really know. Tommy moves around a lot and he doesn't really hang with too many niggas. He works out at Snap Fitness," Cassandra said.

My mind started racing as I listened to Cassandra telling me everything that I wanted to hear. From the things

I heard, it sounded like Tommy was my type of nigga. Paid, handsome, muscled, and did I say paid? The question is, am I his type of woman? Judging by Tia, we both had one thing in common and that was a nice body. I knew that Tommy was certainly an ass man.

Ciara

I was busy at the boutique. My grand opening went great and my entire old customers returned. I even made some new customers. My location was a great choice. I had the perfect spot for people walking or driving by. My window display captured the eyes of many women and they walked in empty handed, but walked out with a bag. London and I put in some work and we were busy for the holiday season. I ordered extra pieces of clothing around this time of year because I didn't want to run out of stock so quickly. A customer never wants to hear sorry, but I no longer have that dress available. I kept the boutique opened one hour extra because of the holiday season. London started working at eleven and closed at eight. I opened at nine and usually left around five thirty. I had to pick the

140

kids up by six p.m., but sometimes Smooth will pick them up for me like he did today. I had to go grocery shopping for Thanksgiving. I was having Thanksgiving dinner at my home and invited everyone. I gathered my things and prepared to leave for the day. I told London goodbye and informed her to call me if she needed me to come back and help her. She assured me that she would be fine. I left and called Smooth.

"Hey honey. How is everything going? What are the kids doing?" I asked.

"Hey bae. We cool and I'm helping them with their homework. Junior has a surprise for you when you come home," Smooth said.

"Oh that's great to hear. I will pick up something to eat on my way home," I said.

"Don't worry about that bae. I picked up a pizza and yes I got your favorite chicken pizza," Smooth said.

"Wow thank you. I see someone is being pretty helpful. Put me on speaker so I can say hello to the kids," I said. Smooth put me on speaker.

"Hey Erica and Junior, mommy will be home in a couple of hours. I love you," I said.

"Okay mommy, love you too." They said.

"I love you too my Blackbone," Smooth said.

"Love you more Mr. Kiss, kiss," I said and smiled as I ended the call.

I made it to Food 4 Less in Melrose Park on 25th and North Avenue. The parking lot was packed. I parked all the way at the end and had to fight for that parking stall. The lady cursed me out and stuck up her middle finger. I didn't care because I was having a good day and wasn't anyone going to stop that. While walking through the parking lot, I grabbed a shopping cart. I didn't want to get to the front door and there wasn't any left. I made it inside and it was a mad house. Thanksgiving was next week and I had to get my shopping done and over with. I pulled out my grocery list and pushed my cart down the aisle. "Here goes," I said to myself. A lady close by laughed and said, "I feel the same way." I laughed and started my grocery shopping. Twenty minutes later and half of the items that I needed on my list I ran into someone that I particular didn't get along

142

with. She was standing in the aisle deciding what seasonings to buy. I invited Vell and her simply because that was his girl. I pushed my cart toward hers and she turned around and looked at me with a frown on her face. 'Does this bitch ever smile?' I thought to myself. I decided to be the bigger person and speak.

"Hi Aaliyah. How are you and the girls doing?" I asked, but was dry as hell.

"Hi Ciara and the twins are doing fine. How are you doing? I know after what happened at the wedding could be very dramatizing," Aaliyah said acting like she really gave a fuck.

"Oh, I'm doing just fine and so is my family. Are you attending my Thanksgiving dinner next week Vell?" I asked.

"Yes, I and my family will be there," Aaliyah said with a fake ass smile on her face.

"Fine, I look forward to seeing the twins," I said and continued to push my cart down the aisle.

I was definitely growing up. I didn't like Aaliyah, but since that was Vell's woman it stopped Kelly and I from getting in that ass. She was such a complainer and so fucking negative. I bet she nagged the hell out of Vell all the time. I didn't like her and didn't trust her. I still invited the bitch to my functions. I believed in keeping your enemies closer and to kill them with kindness. I made a mental note to spit in that bitch food.

I pulled in the garage and Smooth came out to get the bags. Erica and Junior were busy watching television. They didn't even notice that I walked in. I kicked off my shoes and dropped my purse on the kitchen counter. I was so tired.

"Hey mommy's Angels," I said.

They both turned around and ran to hug me. I was so weak that they almost knocked me down. Junior ran over to show me his surprise. It was turkey that he made in daycare and it had Happy Thanksgiving on it.

"This is very nice Junior. Let's go hang it on the fridge," I said.

We went in the kitchen and I placed it on the fridge. Smooth was busying putting the meat in the deep freezer. I told the children to go and finish watching television while I put the groceries away. Smooth walked in and hugged me from behind. He kissed me on my neck and I laughed.

"You ran into Aaliyah in Food 4 Less?" Smooth asked.

"Yes I did. She must have told Vell and he told you," I said.

"Yes, she said you were being snotty as usual," Smooth said laughing.

"Smooth that bitch is lying. I was nice this time and I really surprised myself. I don't have time for her. She's bipolar," I said laughing.

Smooth laughed and sat down at the table. I warmed up my pizza and sat across from him.

"I have so much to do. It seem like this month is going by fast. I can't believe Thanksgiving is next week," I said.

"Why don't you call your mother and my mother and ask them to help you out," Smooth said.

"That's a great idea and Kelly's grandma is baking the cakes and pies. So I have the dessert covered," I said.

"Ciara, we still have to start our counseling. We have been putting it off. It's going on December now," Smooth said.

"I know you're right. I tell you what, why don't you schedule the appointment and I will make myself available," I said.

"Good, I will call tomorrow bae," Smooth said.

I looked over at the children and seen that they had fallen asleep while watching television. I laughed and shook my head and asked Smooth to carry them in their rooms. He got up and took care of his daddy duties. I thought about having a nice sip of wine right now, but it's too risky and Smooth might see me. I ate my pizza and decided to call everyone tomorrow. Besides, I didn't feel like hearing my mother preaching and Smooth's mother voice at the moment.

Thanksgiving Day

Smooth

My house was packed. All my fellas was here, Ant, Vell, and Red. They all bought their girls, Kelly, Aaliyah, and Denise. Their children were there as well. My mother and Ciara's mom Brenda was in the kitchen busy cooking and getting dinner together. I and the men was downstairs in the basement watching football.

"Touchdown! You mutherfuckers better have money tonight. The Bears ain't bullshitting!" Ant screamed.

"Man fuck them sorry ass Bears. It's still early the Broncos still got time to beat they ass," Red said.

"Not going to happen, like I said you better have my money," Ant said passing the blunt to me.

"Shit, Ant is it too late to change my mind?" I asked laughing hitting the blunt.

147

They laughed at me. I bet five hundred that Denver was going to blow Chicago out. Judging by the score me, Red and Vell lost that money. Ant was smiling and grinning. I sat back and talked a lot more shit until my phone vibrated. I looked at who was calling, it was Kayla. I ignored the call and she called me back three more times. I didn't have time to talk to her now. Right now, I was with my family and friends. Not to mention, my girl was upstairs throwing down in the kitchen. I jumped as I watched the Broncos score and now the game was tied.

"Now bitch talk that shit now!" I said to Ant giving Red and Vell a high five.

"Man fuck ya'll! The Bears winning this game," Ant said.

I heard the door open and someone come down the stairs. It was Aaliyah she passed me her phone and walked over to Vell and sat on his lap whispering in his ear. Damn, I knew it was Kayla calling me. I wanted to hang up the phone, but fuck it was too late now.

"Hello, what's up?" I said.

"Smooth don't what's up me! I know you see me calling your fucking phone!" Kayla yelled.

"Look what I tell you about yelling at me? I didn't hear my phone. I'm too busy watching football," I said.

"Who all at your house?" Kayla asked.

"A few people. What's going on with you, Kayla? How you doing?" I asked changing the subject.

"I'm doing miserable and I'm ready to come home Smooth," Kayla said crying.

I walked out the back door where it was quieter. I know being locked up was bad and the fact that it was the holiday it was worse.

"I know Kayla it will be over soon. You just be strong in there and I got you and my seed once you get out. I promise," I said.

Kayla cried into the phone.

I tried my best to sympathize with her. She kept crying and didn't want to hear anything that I was saying. I had my back turned away from the door and I could feel that someone was listening. I turned around to see that Ciara was standing behind me with her hands on her hip.

"Who the fuck are you talking to Smooth?" she said.

"I'm talking to Tommy," I said.

Ciara looked at me and stormed away back in the house. I ended the call and ran behind her almost knocking Aaliyah down. I gave her back her phone and rushed upstairs. No one seemed to notice what was going on. I ran up the stairs and busted threw our bedroom door. Ciara jumped up in my face angry.

"You must think I'm stupid if you think I believe you were talking Tommy. Smooth, I'm just so tired of your bullshit. Who were you talking too?" Ciara said.

"That was Tommy. If you don't believe me, just call and ask him. Damn Ciara its Thanksgiving. I don't have time for all this arguing," I said.

Ciara stormed out the door and went back downstairs. She pulled Kelly to the side to talk to her. Kelly looked over at me and rolled her eyes. I went back downstairs where the fellas were and the game was over.

Ant was busy collecting his money. I peeled off five Ben Franklin's and gave it to him. Moments later we were eating Thanksgiving dinner. I sat next to Ciara and when I spoke with her she didn't say a word. The others picked up on it. So after a while, I just didn't say anything to her. I was so happy when it was over with and everyone left. I turned my phone completely off. I didn't need for Kayla to call me back. The children went to spend the weekend with my mom. Ciara and I was alone and I wanted to talk.

"Ciara are you going to stay mad at me and stop talking to me?" I asked.

"You know what Smooth I'm not mad at you. I'm cool. We can talk," Ciara said being unbothered.

"About earlier, I was really talking to Tommy on the phone. You believe me right?" I said.

"Yes I believe you Smooth with your lying ass," she smirked, "You can forget about our counseling sessions," Ciara said.

"Why would we do that?" I asked.

"Because shit will never change and why waste everyone time. What good is talking about our problems, but things will still remain the same," Ciara said.

Ciara had a bottle of Riesling and poured herself a glass of wine and swallowed it in one gulp. I went to reach for the bottle, but she stepped back and threatened to hit me. The wine glass hit the floor.

"I will bust you upside your head if you touch me!" Ciara said drinking out of the bottle.

I wrestled with her and she was strong. Bam! She busted me upside my head with the wine bottle. I grabbed my head as blood ran down the side of my face. I became dizzy and passed out hitting the floor. I could hear Ciara screaming and crying.

"Oh no! Smooth, I'm so sorry! Smooth, I'm sorry baby!" Ciara cried.

Ciara went to grab a towel and wrapped my head up. She called 911 and explained to the operator what was going on. She applied pressure to my wound until the paramedics arrived.

Chapter Thirteen

Kelly

I couldn't believe that Ciara had busted Smooth upside his head. I don't do the domestic violence, but his ass deserved it. He was disrespectful on Thanksgiving. Ciara told me that she overheard him talking and she could tell by the conversation that it was a female. That nigga ain't shit and I just wish that my best friend would just leave his hoe ass alone. I was on my way to class on this wintery morning. I had on my Northface coat with my hat, gloves, and scarf wrapped around my neck. It was now December and I didn't even start my Christmas shopping yet. The good thing was I made my Christmas list. I had twenty three more days to get everything on it. My brother Shawn was coming home and GG was so happy. I was too I missed my brother so much. He was coming in two weeks and staying at one of his properties. I went to class tired as hell. Ant and I had sex all night. We were doing all types of freaky shit. I'm trying to start new things and besides he deserved it. My man is so good to me and I love him. I know last year we have been through a lot and we're still rocking. I made it to class and grabbed my usual seat. My phone vibrated and it was Ant sending me a text message: Enjoy your day beautiful. It said.

I sent him a message back: Thank you bae and you do the same. I replied back.

Ant replied: I love you.

I love you more. I replied with hearts and kisses.

The professor walked in the door and I put my phone away. I looked at the clock and I can tell that it was going to be a long ass day. I thought of Ant and how long we have been together. I thought about being his wife in the future and having his children. I wanted boys, no girls. I don't know why I didn't want a daughter. Maybe because I was so hardcore inside and I couldn't see myself raising a sassy mouth mini me. I thought about my mother as well and when Shawn came home we needed to go and visit her. I sat in class, but my mind really wasn't there. I was so happy that this was my last year and I will have my bachelors. I wanted to continue to get my masters. I just wanted to get my career going and later on start a family. Hopefully, Ant would be retired from the streets and we could kick back and buy some properties. I'm so happy that he supports me and my dream. I never wanted to work for anyone else. I know once I'm done I would have to work for a realtor for a minute until I start my very own real estate company. I sat back and wondered what Ant was doing.

Ant

I sat at the table counting my money and smoking a blunt. I thought about Kelly and all the freaky things that we did last night. I loved that girl so damn much. I walked over to the safe and grabbed me a stack of money. Today, I was going to buy her Christmas present. I called Red.

"Hey bitch, you ready?" I said through the phone.

"I'm waiting for your lame ass. What's the plan nigga?" Red said.

"Meet me there. I will be there in about forty minutes," I said.

"Alright," Red said hanging up the phone.

I pulled up in front of the place and Red was sitting inside his Jaguar. The bitch looked nice. I jumped out and so did he. I walked past admiring his car.

"Damn bro, I see you pulled the Jag out. The bitch looks nice," I said.

"Yeah, I wanted to take it for a spin today," Red said.

We walked inside the building and waited to get buzzed in. We were in Jewelers Row. Today, I was buying Kelly an engagement ring. I was popping the question on Christmas Eve. Red was there to help me out. I always asked Kelly what type of ring that she liked and I took notes. I wanted to ask Ciara to come with me, but her and Smooth was fighting and shit, so I didn't bothered to ask her. We walked around and Red and I looked at many rings. The lady at the store made suggest that I should get it custom designed. I agreed and decided to get a custom made white gold three stone, princess cut engagement ring. I also added a princess cut band. Red bought Denise some diamond earrings and a diamond bracelet. The jeweler told me that the ring should be ready in seven days. Red left out with his purchases. We went to sit down to eat at Ronnie's Steak House. We called up Smooth and Vell to meet us there. We were sitting down eating when they both walked in. They waitress walked over to take their orders. Red was so busy talking on the phone with Denise so I couldn't talk and say things that I wanted to say. He finally got off the phone with her. I laughed at Smooth's ass looking at the stitches in his head.

"I see Ciara got your ass good," I joked.

We all started laughing loud as hell and some of the people in the restaurant turned around to see what was going on.

"Man fuck ya'll, ain't shit funny," Smooth said rubbing his head.

"I told that man he better stop playing with Ciara. Next time, she's going to kill you," Vell said.

The waitress bought their food over.

"We cool and it's not going to be any next time," Smooth said pouring steak sauce on his steak.

"Check it out. I just bought Kelly's engagement ring. I'm going to pop the question on Christmas," I said.

"Congrats boy, Kelly's a keeper," Smooth said.

"Damn now, I have to hear Aaliyah's mouth. As soon as she finds out that you proposed to Kelly, she's going to be all in my ear," Vell said stuffing his mouth with food.

Red started laughing, "I'm glad I don't have those problems yet man," he said.

"Soon very soon you will. I see Denise has been hanging out with the ladies. It will rub off on her," Smooth said.

"Kelly's my Queen. She's been rocking with me through it all. I trust her and I know she has my back like I have hers. She's smart, beautiful, and sassy. I love her little short ass to death," I said.

"Yep, they don't really make them like that anymore. Once you find a good woman, you have to lock them down," Vell said.

My phone vibrated and it was Kelly calling me. I told the fellas to be quiet. She was calling to talk and to check in with me. That's something that we both do throughout the day. I told her that I was sitting down having lunch with the fellas. She asked me want I wanted for dinner tonight and I told her some meatloaf and mashed potatoes. I asked her how her day was going and she said that it was going pretty cool. All while she talked, I listened to her baby soft voice in the phone. I wasn't listening to the conversation; I just loved to hear her talk. I'm happy that I made the decision today to buy her that ring.

She said in phone, "Ant... Ant...Anthony you hear me talking to you?" Kelly asked.

"Yeah bae. I will see you this afternoon when you make it home," I said snapping out of the trance.

"I love you, Ant," Kelly said.

"I love you too, Kelly," I said hanging up.

They all looked at me at once I got off the phone and started calling me soft. I laughed and told them fuck you that's my baby. We ate our food and talked about the All-

Star Game that was taking place in Texas. We were all going and that was great because we needed to handle some business with Tommy. We paid our bill and left and went our separate ways.

Ciara

London and I were busy at the boutique. It was one p.m. and we still haven't eaten lunch. Kelly walked in and I was happy to see my friend. She was bundled up like a little kid. I laughed at her.

"Girl, you look like a little short kid walking in here," I laughed.

"That wind is so disrespectful. It was bowing my short ass around," Kelly said laughing.

London walked in from the back.

"Hey London," Kelly said.

"Hey Kelly," London said placing the boxes on the floor from the dolly.

"I don't know about you two, but I am starving," I said, "I'm thinking Chipotle," I said.

"Let's go," London and Kelly said.

I closed down the shop and placed my sign in the door telling my customers that I stepped out for lunch. We jumped in Kelly's car since we didn't have to wait too long for it warm up. When we got to Chipotle, it was a long line. Every restaurant in Oak Park was crowded this time of day. London told me what she wanted and gave me her money to order her food. She quickly went to grab us a table while they were available. Kelly and I stood in line and chatted.

"How are you and Smooth doing?" she asked.

"We cool after I had to go there. Why do you have to hit a person upside their head in order for them to act right?" I said.

"I must admit that he deserved it. But, on a serious note, Ciara you have to stop drinking. You see what happened. Someone got hurt. Would you hit him if you were sober?" Kelly asked.

"Yes I would have," I lied and said.

"You a lie and you know it. Ciara, you need to see someone regarding your drinking. Maybe you should do it alone without Smooth," Kelly said.

"You are right. Maybe I should do counseling alone. I think that would be best," I said.

We finally made it to the front of the line and ordered our food. We walked over to sit at the table with London. She was talking on the phone and from over hearing her conversation you can tell that she was talking to a male. I placed her food and money that she had left over in front of her. She ended her phone call telling the caller, "I love you."

"Hmmm, someone has been bitten by the love bug," I said.

"Spill it girlfriend," Kelly said.

"His name is Jay. He and I have been dating since the summer and things are going pretty good," London said.

"That's the guy you were telling me about. He got you blushing and stuff. I'm happy for you, London," I said.

"Girl, sounds like things are going great. You telling him I love you. Let me find out," Kelly said laughing.

London smiled, "You two have to meet him. I'm having something small at my place for New Years. You two have to come. I know that you might have plans, but just come by for a little while just to meet him," London said.

"I will be there and I can't wait to meet him," I said.

"Count me in. I have to meet this man who has you blushing," Kelly said.

We ate our food, laughed, and talked. My phone rang and it was Smooth. Suddenly, I didn't feel too happy again. I was enjoying my lunch with my girls and didn't feel like being bothered, so I ignored his phone call. Kelly dropped me and London off back at the boutique. We went right back to work. Twenty minutes later, a man walked inside carrying a bouquet of beautiful purple roses.

"Hello, can I help you?" I asked.

"Yes I'm looking for Ciara Robinson," the man said.

"I'm Ciara," I said.

"These are for you," the man said.

The young man gave me the bouquet.

"Those are beautiful," London said. She took the card and read it.

"Just to say I love you never seems enough. I've said it so many times. I am afraid you won't understand what I really mean when I say it. How so much feeling, so much adoration can possibly fit into those three little words. But until I find some other way of saying what I feel, then "I love you" will have to do. So no matter how many times I say it, never take it lightly for you are my life, and my only love. I love you more than ever before. Love Eric."

"Awww, that's so sweet. He even said Love Eric and not Smooth," London laughed and said.

I put the bouquet on the counter and smelled the roses. They were beautiful, but that still didn't change the way that I felt about him.

Smooth

I called several times and she didn't answer her phone. I hoped she liked the flowers that I sent to her. After the altercation that occurred, we haven't been seeing eye to eye. We sleep in the same bed, but we back to not having sex. Shit is crazy. I know I fucked up when Ciara over heard me talking to Kayla on the phone. I know that she really doesn't know that it's her, but if I keep being sloppy then she will find out. I need to do a better job at hiding her and making it seem like that she doesn't exist. Ciara still continued to drink. A couple of days ago when Junior wrote on the wall, I went to go and get the Pine Sol. That's when I saw the bottle of wine behind the Pine Sol. I poured it down the drain. When Ciara went back to go and have a drink she noticed that it was missing. She had an attitude all day with me and didn't want to say why. I knew it was because she knew that I found her hiding place and got rid of her wine. I can also tell when she's had a drink because she's cool and nothing gets to her. She acts like she doesn't have a care in the world. The other night when she was helping the children with their homework Erica blurted out, "Mommy, your breath stinks." Ciara got up and went

166

to brush her teeth. It was starting to affect my household and she needed to get help really soon. I talked to my mom about it and she blamed me. I asked her to keep the children right after Christmas until the New Year, so that Ciara and I can have some alone time. She agreed and asked me what I was going to do regarding Kayla. I honestly didn't know what I was going to do, but I really needed to talk with Kayla about some things.

Ciara walked in from work carrying the bouquet of flowers. I can see that she wasn't frowning any more, but she wasn't smiling either. She walked in and kicked off her shoes at the front door.

"Thank you for the flowers. They are beautiful, but if you think some flowers is going to fix everything and make it all go away then you need to think again," Ciara said.

"Ciara, what are you talking about? How many times do I have to tell you that I was talking to Tommy on the phone?!" I said lying.

"Smooth, you are such a liar, but I don't even care anymore. You know if I want to find out the truth I can.

I'm not putting myself through that. I got better things that I can be doing than to be worried about if you're cheating on me. You have the woman that every man wants and you don't appreciate me!" Ciara said.

"What are you talking about, Ciara? I do appreciate you. I'm just tired of all the fighting. You not giving me no pussy. We living in the same house and not even talking. Damn, I just want things back the way like they used to be," I said.

"Act like it then Eric. Be the Eric that I met five years ago. It seem like the more money you make the more drama you build. It's like you keep adding hoe after hoe. First it was Kayla then came Rochelle. So if I feel and think that you were sneaking and talking on the phone with another bitch, then I have every right to," Ciara said.

I stood there and remained quiet, Ciara had a point the money brought along more problems. She wasn't dumb and she knew that I was fucking around, but it's a good thing that she didn't know it was Kayla. I walked over to her to give her a hug.

"Smooth, you can keep your hugs. I don't want you to touch me. I just hate you," Ciara said.

"I love you, Ciara. Please don't hate me. How can we get back like we used to be?" Smooth asked.

"It takes loyalty, respect, and honesty, Smooth. Those things that you no longer capable of giving me," Ciara said.

She walked away and went upstairs. I went downstairs in the basement and let Ciara have her space. Besides, I wasn't sleeping another night in the bed with Ciara and not getting no pussy. I was getting tired of chasing her ass and I was getting tired of Kayla's ass too. Sometimes I just want to get a new bitch and start the fuck all over. These bitches getting on my nerves.

Chapter Fourteen

Christmas Eve

Kelly

Shawn is back home in Chicago and GG is cooking all his favorite food. I'm so happy that my brother is back home for the holidays. I don't know why I feel so funny, but I can honestly say that I am happy and don't have no drama in my life. The beginning of this year was crazy with the fighting, baby mama drama, kidnappings, and death. I know we have a few days left of this year, but I am truly blessed to say that I don't want to bring all that bullshit into the New Year. I'm leaving all that in the past. GG pressured me to attend church on a regular and I think that I would give it a try. I'm just the type of person that can't sit in church with a bunch of hypocrites. That was my opinion. GG was in the kitchen standing over the stove stirring the caramel for the cake. I walked in and asked if she needed help.

"GG, do you need any help?" I asked.

"Kelly, yes grandma needs all the help that she can get. I need you to grab the cast iron skillet and start making the cornbread. Don't forget to add the buttermilk," GG said.

I did what I was told to do and made my grandma's cornbread recipe. I poured it in the skillet and placed it in the oven. GG was finishing up the caramel cake. I noticed that the onions needed to chop and the potatoes need to be peeled. I went to work in the kitchen.

"Kelly, I see you and Anthony are really growing together," GG said.

"Yes grandma, I love Ant and I really can't see myself with anyone else," I said.

"That's love for you. Sometimes it will sneak up on you. I really like Anthony, he's a good boy," GG said.

I smiled at that comment. It was a point of time in my life when she never like any boy that I introduced her to. I don't know why she talking about me and Ant something must be going on. I do know that Ant came by hear earlier and he and Shawn are together right now handling business.

I continued to move around the kitchen and help GG prepare dinner.

"How is Ciara and Eric doing?" GG asked.

"Well honestly grandma those two are having a lot of problems right now," I said.

"If you ask me, Ciara needs to leave him alone. She can do much better. There is a good man out there for her. Eric isn't ready for a commitment. You can see and feel it. He may be fooling her, but he's not fooling me," GG said.

"You know I tell Ciara plenty of times to drop him. Anthony tells me to stay out of it, so now I don't speak too much on him. Instead, I talk around him and just give my friend some encouragement," I said.

"That's all that you can do. One thing that I do know is, when Ciara is ready to leave him, she will. She has to be the one willing to do it," GG said.

I listened to the advice that my grandma was giving. She wiser and older and been through it. For now on starting the New Year, I was staying out of it and focusing on my relationship. Yes Ciara is my friend and I will be there for her and the children. As far as Smooth, she can forget about it. He was cool and I remember once upon a time I called him my brother, but not anymore. I love my girl Ciara like a sister and if she hurts I hurt. I know things can get messy with him and Ant being one of his best friends. I just stay in my place and don't let it go there and cause a rip in their friendship. I'm just happy that I can trust Ant and know that everyone isn't alike and that he actually has good intentions. Smooth is letting that money get to his head and not thinking about his family. I bet any type of money that he is still involved with that hoe ass Kayla. Let's keep it real Kayla is doing his time. It's no secret that when the Feds came in her house and found all that shit it was Smooth's that she was working for. He was fucking with her then and has never stopped. I know Smooth and he ain't the type of man to leave anyone hanging. Especially, someone who is doing a year for him and hasn't said a word. Ciara underestimates Kayla by calling her slow and stupid and saying that Smooth is just using her. Actually, if it wasn't for Kayla, Smooth wouldn't have been living good last year. Smooth will be in jail doing time. Kayla put in that work in the streets and I give her that much credit.

Ciara calls her all types of hoes, which I do agree. The fact that she is doing time for Smooth shows how loyal she is to him and that all that matters. I just hope that Ciara wakes up one day from the bad nightmare that she is having and leave Smooth's trifling ass alone. Two hours later, everything was cooked and finished in the kitchen. I went home so that I could get ready and come back over tonight. On my way home, Denise called me and I asked if she was coming over for dinner tonight. She said that she would be there with Red. I made it home and quickly undressed and ran my bath water. Ciara called my phone to talk and complain about Smooth, but I cut that conversation short and told her to fuck Smooth and to work on herself. I can tell that she caught a slight attitude, but I didn't give a damn. I wasn't trying to hear all that drama right now. I soaked in the tub and thought what the hell Ant and my brother Shawn were doing. I got out the table and sat on the bed naked and was about to call Ant, but he walked in.

"Hey bae. I made it home just in time," Ant said.

"Ant your hands are cold. You just came in from outside. Where my brother at?" I said.

174

"He's at the hotel getting ready. Can I have some before we leave?" Ant said.

"Ant just a quickie. You know we have to be there in an hour. And you still have to get ready," I said.

"I won't take long, I promise," Ant said.

Two hours later after having sex, Ant and I was preparing for the night and we were finally ready. Both of our phones were blowing up and everyone was asking where we were. I text my brother Shawn to tell him that we were on our way. Once we arrived, everyone was there and was talking and mingling. Ciara was there and so was Smooth, Denise and Red, Vell but minus Aaliyah. He said that Aaliyah was sick and couldn't make it. I already knew that Aaliyah wasn't showing up at anything that I threw. I didn't care for her and didn't hide it either. She rubs me the wrong way and I don't trust her. I don't say shit to her and if we are at the same function I keep my distance. Anthony joined the guys and I went over to join the ladies. A few of GG friends were there and so was many other people that we knew. It was getting late and time to serve dinner. The ladies sat the table and we all took our seats and the huge dining room table. GG said grace over the food.

"God of all gifts, we thank you for the many ways you have blessed us this day. We are grateful each of those who are gathered around this table. We ask you to bless us and our food and to bless those who are not with us today. In our gratitude and love, we remember your humble birth into our lives and pray for those who are without enough to eat. We remember the stable in which you were born and pray for those who have no place to live. We remember you challenging message of caring and giving and we pray for peace in families and nations throughout the world. We bless you and give you thanks in your spirit who brings our hearts to life the Christmas Day and forever. Amen."

Everyone said Amen and starting eating. I made Anthony's plate and piled on the food. Even though he was skinny and tall, Ant could eat. Denise made Red's plate. Ciara made her plate and wasn't going to make Smooth's plate. GG whispered something in her ear and she got up to fix his plate. Everyone ate and talked at the dinner table. It felt good to be surrounded by the people who you loved and loved you. I went over to join Shawn as he sat there alone. I could tell that he had someone on his mind.

"You thinking about Jasmine?" I asked.

"Yes Sis, I miss her so much. I wish she was here with us today," Shawn said.

"I miss her too. Before you leave, we will visit her. We also need to visit mom as well," I said.

I sat there and talked with my brother and Ant walked over to me. Everyone got quiet and all eyes were on us. Ant got down on one bended knee. I covered my face up. I couldn't believe my eyes. I know he was not about to propose to me. Ant went inside his pocket and pulled out a ring box. I starting crying.

"I was in love with you the day I looked into your eyes and completely melted. I love your squeaky voice. Your sassy mouth. And your feisty ways. You touch me in a way no one else has and give me so many reasons to love you. You're the first thing I think of each morning when I wake, you're the last thing I think of each night when I close my eyes. You're in every thought I have and every breath I take. My feelings are growing stronger with every move I make. I love you. Kelly, will you marry me?" Ant asked.

"Yes Anthony, I will marry you," I cried.

Anthony slid the ring on my finger and I fell in his arms. We both kissed as everyone watched and clapped. I knew something felt weird, but it felt right. Everyone rushed over to hug the both of us. They didn't seem surprised at all and knew that Ant was going to propose. I didn't have the slightest clue. Ant tricked me real good. GG kissed and hugged Ant.

"You better take good care of my baby," GG said.

"Don't worry GG, I will. I promise to love her," Ant said.

It was getting late and everyone prepared to leave. I was so blessed that I was engaged to the man that I truly love and I knows that he truly loves me. I was so happy to his wife and to grow old with him. We have been through some things and throughout everything Ant and I are still rocking. I loved that man and wouldn't trade him for nothing in the world. We thanked everyone and celebrated.

I will never forget this moment and this is the best gift that I've ever received and the best Christmas I've ever had.

Shawn

I was home celebrating the holidays and handling business. I was leaving in a few days right before New Year's. During my visit, I talked and starting doing business with Ant. He was the first person that I could think of when it came to getting money. I hollered at him about the some properties that were for sell in California. I needed a partner to go in on buying a few. The properties were twice more expensive than Chicago. I knew that we could make a killing once we bought them. I sat with him and told him the game plan and assured him that he will get double back in money within a year. Ant agreed, but he wanted to see the properties first and take a trip to Cali before he gave up any money. That was fair and alright with me. I was ready to make it happen and to get the ball rolling and get this money. I was through the streets of Chicago and seen a few buildings that were for sale. I wonder what they wanted for them, but then again I thought if I really wanted to start back buying things here. I put everything in Kelly's name here and gave her full control. So far she's been holding it down and doing a pretty good job. I was really proud of my sister and happy that she will be graduating from college and getting married. Kelly was receiving the one thing that anyone can't take away and that was her Bachelor's Degree. I remember the day I started hustling. GG wasn't happy and was worried about me being out the streets of Chicago. I was fine and I could hold my own down. I was getting tired of seeing GG struggle and take care of us with her little social security check. Both of our parents were locked up and Kelly was shop lifting. I just wanted to make money and change my family's situation. I remember some of the members of GG's church talking bad about Kelly and me. She was upset and she didn't let them speak badly of us. Despite every bad thing that we did, GG has always been by our side. I continued to hustle and bring money home. Now, GG doesn't have to worry about nothing. I pay her bills and make sure that the property taxes are paid. I put Kelly through school because I didn't want her to depend on anyone out her. I wanted her to make her own money and to become successful. Kelly never planned on continuing her education after high school. When I introduced her to this black real estate woman that I knew, she told her how easy it was to make money she changed her mind. Seeing her going to school, also made GG very happy and proud of her granddaughter. Now, all the church folks do is talk about how we're doing good now. I didn't care what anyone had to say about me. I was getting out here every day and making it happen. I thought about Jasmine every day. After her death, I had to relocate and leave Chicago. I feel as though I am to blame for her and Nisha's death. I made way up to the cemetery. When I got there, I sat in the car for a moment. I got out and walked through the snow and fought the wind to get to her plot. The picture of Jasmine looked beautiful on her tombstone. I cried as I stood in front of her grave. I began to talk to her.

"Jasmine, I miss you so much. I think about you all the time. I want to say that I'm truly sorry for all the bad things that I did to you. I was a fool and I didn't know any better. I didn't know that I had such a wonderful woman in my life. I'm sorry that I played with your heart back and forth. I loved you and I'm sorry that I didn't love you as hard as you loved me. I will give anything to have you back

181

in my life. I wish that I could turn back the hands of time. Please forgive me, Jasmine," I cried.

I stood outside as it started to snow again. The tears ran down my face. I was frozen and couldn't move. It wasn't because of the temperatures it was because I felt as though I wasn't done talking. I touched her tombstone as if I was touching her. I could hear someone walking towards me. I turned around to see who was approaching me and it was Kelly.

"I knew that you were here," Kelly said.

She could see that I have been crying. I tried to clean my face and hide the tears. Kelly stood by me and rubbed my back. She starts crying as well. We both stood out in the cold talking to Jasmine.

"Hey sis guess what Antony proposed to me. I remember you telling me that he and I were going to be together. I remember playing like I didn't like him knowing that I really did. And now we are getting married. I wish you were here to be my brides mate. I really miss you and I know that you still are with us. I love you, sis," Kelly cried.

We both hugged one another and walked back to our cars. Kelly pulled off before me and I followed behind her. We parked her car in front of GG's place. GG came outside the house and I opened the door for her and she got inside the car. It was me, Kelly, and GG in route and on the road to visit my mother in prison. This is GG's first time ever going to visit my mother while she's been upstate. My mother never took her name off the list. I know that she was going to extremely happy to see GG. We got there in three hours and it took another forty-five minutes to go through the process. The guards called our names and we went through the doors and sat down at the table. Everyone waited for the guards to bring the inmates out for their visitations. The doors clicked and unlocked. One by one, the female inmates walked out. We sat there and waited and out comes my mother looking like a different person. She gained weight, her skin was flawless, and her hair was in a long ponytail down her back.

"Momma, is that you?" Kelly said.

My mother and Kelly hugged and she noticed Kelly's engagement ring on her finger and smiled. She hugged me next and kissed me on my forehead just like she used to do when I was a little boy. When it came to GG, my mother stood there. GG grabbed her and hugged her so tight. They both cried.

"Happy New Year daughter. I love you and I miss you," GG cried.

Chapter Fifteen

New Year's Eve

London

I was having a small gathering at my house for New Year's Eve, nothing too big. I really didn't have the space. My tiny little condo that I lived in Berwyn couldn't hold any more than twenty people. I had everything prepared and what you needed for a party. I had Drake playing in the background I stood in front of my closet deciding on what to wear tonight. I was interrupted by the ringing off my phone and seen that it was Jay's face calling me. I only had on my bra and boy shorts. I answered his call.

"Hello Mr.," I said in my sexy voice.

"Wow! It looks like I called you at the right time. Let me see you baby," Jay said.

I moved my phone around so that Jay could have a better view of my body.

"Can you see me now?" I asked.

"Yes you look so tasty. I can't wait to see you tonight sexy," Jay said.

"I can't wait to see you either J," I said.

"What are you doing? You like walking around the house in your underwear?" Jay asked.

"Yes I do. But, I was trying to decide which dress to wear tonight. Are you bringing anyone with you?" I said.

"Yes, I'm bringing one of my buddies with me. I'm sure that you would look good in whatever that you decide to wear," Jay said.

"Thank you handsome. I can't wait to bring in the New Year with you," I said.

"I can't wait to bring in it with you as well beautiful. I will check back on you later and I love you," Jay said.

"Okay, love you too," I said blowing kisses.

I ended the call and thought about the moment we met. We met in June. I was at one of my friend's annual yacht party that he has every year. He had catered food, Jet Ski's, and a live DJ. I was enjoying myself in my green two piece bikini. The weather was a hot and steamy ninety degrees. Everyone was in the water getting wet. I hopped on the Jet Ski and joined everyone in the water. Once I got out of the water, I applied more suntan lotion and off bug spray to my skin. I felt like someone was watching me so I looked over my shoulder. I noticed this guy looking at me. He smiled and I smiled back and continued to oil my body. I made way over to the bar and ordered myself a drink. When it was time to pay for my drink, I heard a man say, 'Don't worry, I will pay.' I looked behind me and it was the guy that I smiled at.

"Thank you, but you didn't have to pay for my drink," I said politely.

"No the pleasure is all mine beautiful. I'm Jay and who am I having the pleasure of speaking to?" Jay said.

"I'm London and nice to meet you," I said.

"London, are you single?" Jay asked.

"Yes I am. Are you single?" I asked looking at his hand for a ring.

"Yes I am. Don't worry, I'm not married," Jay said laughing.

"You never know now days. I'm just making sure," I said.

"Can we exchange numbers and I would love to take you out on a date," Jay said.

"Sure that would be nice," I said.

Jay and I exchanged numbers. We talked a week on the phone getting to know one another. Jay was twenty five and single with no children. He was an Engineer and had a Master's Degree in Engineering. He stayed downtown alone. He didn't eat pork. He loved to have fun and was very athletic. Jay was fine and had a great body. He kind of reminded me of Nelly, but minus the country slang. We went on our first date at Del Frisco's. It was lovely and we both had Filet Mignon, Lobster Macaroni and Cheese, and Asparagus with Martini's. Dinner was great and I really enjoyed myself. Jay was such a gentleman and treated me like a lady. A month into our relationship, we had done a lot of things together like rock climbing and sky diving. He showed me things that another man hasn't and we had so much fun. Jay asked me to be his woman and I said yes. Once ninety days hit, I had sex with him. We were at his place downtown. I was horny and ready. Before I met him, I haven't had sex in six months. Jay blew my back out and knocked the cobwebs off my pussy. He treated my pussy with care. After having sex, we grew closer than before. I found my freaky partner and sex was exciting. I also realized that we had a deeper connection and that's what made me love him even harder. I still remember the day when he first told me that he loved me. We were at the Fright Fest at Six Flags Great America on the Ragin' Cajun and after the ride was over he told me that he loved me. Meeting Jay has been an amazing thing in my life. I was starting to thinking that chivalry didn't exist anymore. When I met him, he showed me that it was still some respectful men out here. In my past, I would meet men he loved to show me off in public and acted like they were crazy about me. But behind closed doors they were crazy as hell and didn't care about me. It went from having sex to making love. Jay was different and when you see us out together in public being lovey dovey. You better believe that it was turned up ten times more behind closed doors. I

189

couldn't wait till see him tonight and bring in the New Year with him. It was going down and I was so anxious.

Ciara

I bounced up and down on top of Smooth. Yes, we were back having sex, but it was only because I had needs and wanted to fuck. I still was feeling Smooth and his shady ways, but as long as he was here he was going to be good for something. The sex was basic and boring, no head, and I made his ass strap up. I don't know who Smooth was fucking on the side and we all know that his ass would go in a bitch raw. I got my orgasm and was ready to stop fucking, but Smooth wouldn't let me. He rolled over on top of me and pinned me down.

"Smooth, get off of me!" I said as I tried to fight him.

"Hell nawl. You got me fucked up if you think you just going to fuck me and I don't nut," he said.

Smooth pumped in and out of me, pounding in my pussy. It hurt so bad and was painful. I moaned in pain and tried to close my legs shut.

"Ciara, why you fighting me? Take this dick and it won't be hard," Smooth said.

I stopped fighting and just let him have his way. He fucked me harder and it was pleasurable and painful. I hated his ass so much, but he had my pussy creaming again. Judging by the vein popping out the side of his head, I knew he was ready to bust. He pumped faster and let out a growl. Smooth's sweaty body collapsed on top of me. I pushed his ass off of me and went to get in the shower.

"Ciara bring me a towel," Smooth said.

"I'm not bringing you shit," I said and walked off.

I was slow because my legs and pussy was sore thanks to him. I couldn't get in the tub, so I ran some bath water instead. I was on the toilet pissing when Smooth walked in the bathroom.

"Didn't I tell you to bring me a towel?" he said.

I ignored him because I didn't feel like arguing today. Smooth cleaned his dick off and went to lie down in bed. I soaked in the tub and relaxed. I was still planning on going to London's New Year's gathering. I wasn't taking Smooth with me. I don't know what he had planned, but I didn't make any plans with him this year. I got out of the tub and walked in the room. He was snoring and I wanted to smack the shit out of his ass in his sleep. I threw on my robe and went downstairs to be alone. The children were over at Smooth's mother house bringing in the new year with her. I went out in the garage and got my little personal bottle of wine. I gulped it down and went back inside. I promise that tonight was my last night of me drinking. Starting the New Year, I was getting help. Smooth was still in the bed sleep. I was hungry so I ordered Chinese food from the restaurant. Smooth hated Chinese food. Oh well, he could cook his self-something to eat. I turned on the television and watched Breaking Bad on Netflix. I was chilling and enjoying the show. The doorbell rang and it was my food. I was in the kitchen putting my food on the plate when Smooth came down.

"Who was at the door, babe?" he asked.

192

"My Chinese food that I ordered for me to eat," I said.

"You know I don't like Chinese food. What am I supposed to eat?" Smooth said.

"I don't know and really don't care," I said walking back to sit down on the couch.

"That's what we on now? Everyone for themselves now. Ciara, you acting real immature right now," Smooth said.

I ignored his ass and watched television and ate my food. Smooth came in the living room and knocked my plate out of my hand and turned off the television.

"What the fuck is wrong with you?" I yelled.

"You are what's wrong. I'm getting tired of your mutherfucking attitude and your smart ass mouth. I don't know who the fuck you think you playing with Ciara. You making me start to hate you," Smooth said.

I jumped up in his face and stood on tiptoes.

"Fuck you, Smooth and you're the reason why I'm acting like this. I'm not feeling this anymore. I want you out of my house and out of my life!" I yelled.

"I'm not going no mutherfucking where! We going to sit down and talk this shit out like adults, Ciara. We both have a family to raise. Sit your ass down, Ciara," Smooth said.

I tried to walk off. He grabbed me by the arm and slanged me over on the couch. I fell across the couch and my robe opened up exposing my naked body. My hair was no longer in a ponytail. I sat on the couch with my face balled up.

"Talk to me Ciara. Why are we fighting? I don't want to fight you, bae," Smooth said.

"Smooth, I'm going to ask you this question and I want you to tell me the truth," Ciara said.

"Go head what's the question? I'm listening," Smooth said.

"Are you seeing, fucking, or entertaining other bitches?" I asked.

"No, I'm not Ciara. Why do you keep accusing me of cheating on you?" Smooth asked.

"You know the fuck why. Since when does a man have to step outside to take a phone call?" I said.

"I told you I was talking to Tommy. I stepped outside to talk on the phone because it was too much noise in the house," Smooth said.

"Yeah whatever nigga, tell me anything," I said.

"I'm telling you the truth, Ciara. I love you and only want to be with you. How many times do I have to tell you that?" Smooth said.

I rolled my eyes and sat on the couch and listened while he fed me those lies.

London

Everyone was enjoying themselves. Ciara and Kelly arrived. I could tell something wasn't quite right with Ciara. I made a mental note to myself to talk with her later. Kelly was all smiles and bubbly. I gave them a quick tour of my condo. The last room that I showed them was my bedroom.

"Thank you both for coming. Let me give you a tour," I said to Ciara and Kelly.

I excused myself from my other guests.

"Congratulations Kelly on your engagement. Your ring is beautiful. I'm so happy for you and Anthony," I said.

"Thank you Hun. I wish you would've been there. How was your Christmas?" Kelly asked.

"I know I wish I was there as well. My Christmas was great. I spent it with Jay and his family," I said.

"How were they?" Ciara asked.

"They were fine. I had to put on my good girl role," I said laughing.

"London, I love your condo it's very lovely," Kelly said.

"Thank you Kelly. I wish I could take all the credit for being creative and coming up with my own designs, but

196

I can't. Girl, I copied everything from the O magazine," I said laughing.

The three of us laughed.

"I love it and it's you and your style," Ciara said.

"Thank you ladies," I said.

We walked back out to join the rest. Before I approached the rest of my guests, I pulled Ciara to the side.

"Hey Ciara, are you fine? It seems like something is bothering you," I said.

"Really, you can tell? I'm fine, Smooth and I am just going through some things at the moment," Ciara said.

"Yes, I can tell when you're going through something. I'm your friend and if you ever need to talk, I'm here to listen. Now, you need to shake it off because you making me sad," I said.

"Thank you London for being a true friend," Ciara said giving me a hug.

"Anytime, now let's turn up girl. Don't let any man steal your joy," I said.

My guests starting arriving and more people showed up than I expected, but it was fine. I was waiting for Jay to arrive. I don't know why I felt nervous like a young high school girl. No man has ever made me feel this way before. Jay sent me a text saying that he was looking for a parking place. I went in my bedroom and spritz my body with perfume and applied more lip gloss to my lips. I looked in my mirror and made sure that the red tight fitted dress was okay. My dress hugged my curves and Jay was crazy about my curves. I could hear voices coming from upfront over the music. I over heard someone say hello and that London stepped in back, but will be out shortly. I waited five more minutes than made my grand entrance. I walked out and Jay eyes were glued on me. He was standing next to dark skin guy.

"Hey babe, I'm so glad that you are finally here," I said hugging Jay.

"You look beautiful babe. You know that I wouldn't miss anything that you throw," Jay said.

We were wrapped in each other's arms. Our eyes were locked on one another. We zoned everyone out and felt like we were the only ones in the room. Someone cleared their throat to get our attention.

"Excuse me. I hate to bring this up, but I'm Kanye, Jay's friend," Kanye said.

"My fault man, baby this is my friend Kanye. Kanye this is the love of my life, London," Jay said.

"Nice to meet you, London," Kanye said.

"Nice to meet you too. Let me introduce the both of you to my friends," I said.

Ciara and Kelly were off to the side smiling and waiting to be introduced.

"Jay this is Ciara and Kelly. Ciara and Kelly this is Jay and his friend Kanye," I said.

"Hello, finally nice to meet you, Jay. London talks about you all the time. Nice meeting you as well Kanye," Ciara said shaking their hands.

"Hello, Jay and Kanye," Kelly said.

"Hello to you Ciara. I hope that it's all good things," Jay said laughing.

We all laughed. I noticed Kanye looking at Ciara as she spoke and smiled. I could tell that he was feeling her. I offered everyone appetizers and some something to drink. Jay and I went off to be alone. We excused ourselves and went in my bedroom for some privacy. As soon as I stepped inside, Jay closed and locked the door. He lifted me up and placed me on top of my dresser. My dress was hiked up and his big hands caressed my thighs as we kissed.

"You look so mutherfucking good right now. You got my dick so damn hard," Jay said in between kisses. I grabbed his dick and yes he was rock hard. I jumped off the dresser and pushed him back on my bed. I straddled him and my pussy was so wet that he slid inside me.

Meanwhile back in the living room, Ciara and Kanye were getting better acquitted.

"Ciara, do you mind if I ask you a question?" Kanye asked.

"No, I don't mind at all," Ciara said.

"Are you single?" Kanye asked.

"I'm not single, but my relationship is going left, instead of right at the moment," Ciara said.

"I see. Is it fine that I leave you my number? I would love if you would call me and I can take you out to dinner one day," Kanye.

"That is fine," Ciara said.

Kanye and Ciara both exchanged numbers. Kelly was talking across the room and noticed the both of them. Ciara was smiling from ear to ear. She was happy to see her best friend getting back out there.

"About time my girl is getting herself a dip on the side," Kelly said in her mind.

Kelly walked over to Ciara after Kanye walked off.

"Girl, I see you over here being bad. I love it. He's fine and you better call his ass too," Kelly said.

"Yes, he is fine. I don't know if I'm going to call him, but I will have him on standby," Ciara smiled and said.

"I feel you and look at these two freaky ones walking out of the bedroom like they just didn't get finished having sex," Kelly laughed.

Jay and I walked back out to join our party. I went over to Ciara and Kelly. They both said that they had to leave and get back home to bring in the New Year with their man. Kelly's phone rang and I could tell that it was Anthony on the other line. She smiled into the phone and told him that she was on her way home. Ciara's phone rang and the fact that she didn't answer let me know that it was Smooth calling her. After the second call, she accepted it. She had an unpleased look across her face. I heard her tell Smooth that she was leaving and that she would be in the house shortly. Ciara was snappy on the phone. I couldn't wait to have a private talk with her to find out what the hell was going on. I hugged them both and thanked them for coming to my gathering.

"Thank you Ciara and Kelly for coming. Happy New Year and enjoy the rest of the night," I said.

"Thanks for inviting us. Jay is really nice and you both make a lovely couple," Ciara said.

"Yes you do and I see how you two sneaked off to have a quickie," Kelly said laughing.

"Thank you and yes quickies are fun," I said laughing.

We laughed and I walked them to the door. They said goodbye to Jay and Kanye. Kelly walked out the door while Ciara slowed down and gave Kanye a hug.

"It was a pleasure meeting you Miss Ciara. Don't forget to use my number," Kanye said.

"Thank you and the feeling is mutual. I will call you when I get a chance," Ciara said.

I looked at Kelly and she was smiling. What the hell did I miss? I can't wait to talk to Miss Ciara when I get a chance. I guess her and Smooth are really having trouble in paradise. I closed the door and went back to entertaining my guests. Truthfully, I was ready for it to be over so I could be alone with Jay. I was happy to be bringing it in with him.

Smooth

While Ciara was out, Kayla called me. The last time we talked was last week and the call was cut short when Ciara made it home. I told Kayla that she needed to hit my line during the hours that Ciara was working. It was like she was calling me during the hours when Ciara was around to start some bullshit on purpose. I know one thing I'm not going to allow, and that is letting Kayla disrespect the fact that I am with Ciara. That's why in the fuck everything is so shaky now. I answered her call.

"What's up, Kayla? Aye, why you being so hard headed and not calling during the hours that I told you? You on that some ole bullshit. Starting shit and disrupting my household," I said.

"Smooth, I don't know what the hell you talking about. I call you when I can talk. You know by me being pregnant that I have to attend classes that are during the day. So once I'm free that is when I call you. Don't come at me about disrupting your fucking household. I'm pregnant by you. What about this mutherfucking household in my stomach!" Kayla said.

"Look, I told you that I got you. I take care of all my seeds. You and the baby ain't got to worry about shit just be mindful of the times you call me. If I don't pick up my phone, that means I can't talk. So you don't have to keep calling my phone back to back. Another thing, don't have Aaliyah calling for you either. If I see that she calls me, I'm ignoring her calls too," I said.

"Smooth you got me fucked up. This is what's going to happen. When I call your phone, you will answer. I don't care if you talk in code, but you better answer your damn phone. I'm here pregnant and locked up anything can happen. You act like I talk to you every day. I need to hear from you once during the week and I will call you on Saturday because I know Sunday you will be with your family. If you don't answer your phone, then I will be giving Ciara a call and talk to her since you don't have time to talk," Kayla said.

"Kayla, you like starting shit. If you ever think about calling Ciara and starting shit, you can forget about ever calling or getting in touch with me again. Remember, you don't have anywhere to live when you get out. Play with me if you want to and your ass would get played at the end," I said.

"Smooth, fuck you and I'm not trying to argue with you right now. I'm six months pregnant carrying your child and not to mention, did you forget the reason while I'm up in here in the first place? We not going to go there though. Let's just sweep that part underneath the rug. Smooth, you have some nerve to try and threaten me. If it wasn't for me, you know what I'm not going to go there over this phone. You better respect me and act like you got some fucking sense," Kayla said.

"Alright, I'm tired of fighting. Hell, I already gotta hear Ciara's mouth so when I talk to you I expect a different tone. How is the baby doing?" I asked.

"She's doing fine. My breast are getting bigger and I'm having morning sickness. I can't hold anything down, but potatoes. So I just eat mashed potatoes, fries, chips, etc. Other than that I'm fine and just ready to be free," Kayla said.

"That's good to hear. It will be over with soon just hang in there," Smooth said.

206

"August seems so far away from now. I'm just counting down the time for our baby to arrive in April," Kayla said.

"I told my mother about you being pregnant. Would it be fine if my mother kept our daughter instead of Aaliyah?" Smooth asked.

"That's not a problem. After all, she is the grandmother and could give more attention to our baby. Aaliyah already has her children to tend to. Having your mother raise our baby would be perfect," Kayla said.

"I agree as well. That's why I asked her," Smooth said.

"Okay, I will tell Aaliyah that your mom will take my baby once she's born. (Yawn) I'm sleepy, me and the baby about to lay it down for the night. Happy New Year and I will call you back on Saturday. You not going out tonight to celebrate?" Kayla said.

"No, I'm staying in this year and chilling. Get you some rest and call me around the afternoon Saturday. Happy New Year to you as well," I said.

I got off the phone just in time because I could hear Ciara pulling into the garage. I watched television as she strolled in. She was looking cute in her black jumpsuit. I decided to stay in for the New Year. It was safer and I wanted to bring it in with the person that I loved. I know I just got off the phone with Kayla, but I wasn't in love with her. Really, no other woman could ever take the place of Ciara, that's why when she puts up a fight I deal with it. Stick it out and don't leave. Me and that girl has been through so much and still had a lot to go through. She rolled her eyes as she walked passed me. I tried to smack her on the ass.

"Smooth don't touch my ass. You lost that privilege," Ciara said sitting down to take off her boots.

"That's my ass and will always be. I can touch it whenever I like. Let me help you take off your boots," I said.

I pulled each one of Ciara's boots off. I rubbed her feet as she kicked back and relaxed.

"How was London's New Year's party? Was anyone trying to talk to you?

"It was a gathering and no didn't anyone try to talk to me. Why would you ask me something like that?" Ciara said.

"I'm asking because tonight my baby looks so good in her jumpsuit. You're beautiful. If it was my first time seeing you, I know that I would try to holler at you. Especially, with all that ass," I said.

"Well you got me and you still try to holler at other women too. I guess my pretty face and big ass isn't good enough. How do you explain that Smooth?" Ciara said.

"I don't try to holler at no damn body. I only want you. I love you, Ciara," I said.

"Whatever Smooth and I love your hoe ass too," Ciara said.

I continued to rub her feet and ignored her last comment of her calling me a hoe. Truthfully, I didn't feel like I was a hoe. I wasn't out here trying to sleep with everyone. Kayla was actually before her and so was Rochelle. At the time when I was dealing with them, it was only about sex. Rochelle was cool, but she was money

209

hungry and that shit gets you nowhere with me. Kayla was sneaky and crazy as hell. She was also money hungry, but she was willing to listen and easy to manipulate. Kayla worked with feelings and Rochelle didn't have feelings for me. She was just ready to settle and didn't want me to be with Ciara. Kayla doesn't care about being on the side as long as you take care of her. If you ignore her, things could get messy, but now that she needs me she really wouldn't try a lot of crazy shit. The moment I met Ciara, I could tell that she was different. What's crazy is that she is younger than both Kayla and Rochelle. The fact that she had to take care of herself when she was younger made her a fighter and stronger. Wasn't anything given to her. She wasn't chasing men to get a dollar. What I loved the most is she wasn't lazy, a follower, or out in the streets. Ciara was a rose in the concrete which is rare to find. The situation with Rochelle was a fucked up situation. This situation with Kayla is even worse. I was using condoms with her and she still ended up pregnant. I was extra cautious with Kayla, but ain't no erasing it now, I have another child on the way and I have to deal with it. I know when Ciara finds out that it's going to crush her and I could lose her forever.

Chapter Sixteen

Aaliyah

It was the third week in January and I had to go and visit my girl Kayla. I haven't been able to really talk to her because I was so busy running around for the holiday season. I cleared up my schedule and made my way downtown. I sat in the visiting room and watched Kayla walk out with her cute little belly.

"Hey girl. You look so cute pregnant," I said rubbing her belly.

"Hey Aaliyah, thank you. Girl, I'm just ready to have my little lady," Kayla said.

"You want something from the vending machine?" I asked.

"Yes chips are fine and some water," Kayla said.

I went to the vending machine and placed the card inside to purchase our junk food. That shit was high in there, but I had to make sure that we had enough snacks for our visit. I sat back down and was ready to fill Kayla in on all the juicy gossip.

"Have you been talking to Smooth?" I asked.

"Yes, we've been talking. I had to go off on his ass. He felt like I was on some messy shit every time that I called him, saying I call during the hours when Ciara is around. I told his ass fuck him and Ciara. He worried about her finding out and shit. He worried about the wrong shit. When he need to be worried about me and my damn baby," Kayla said.

"He gotta be talking about the time when you called him on Thanksgiving and I gave him the phone. Ciara caught his ass on the phone too. I don't know what exactly what she said to Smooth, but her face was balled up during the rest of the night. It was obvious that she was upset. That shit was funny. I enjoyed every bit of seeing her unhappy," I said.

"I'm surprised you went to the dinner. Who all was there? How is their house?" Kayla asked.

"Girl, Vell made me go because I really didn't want to be there. You know all the guys were there. Ant and Red along with Kelly and Red's new girlfriend, Denise, Ciara and Smooth's mothers, and the children were there too. I'm not going to hate, but they house is nice and spacious. I didn't get a tour, but the first floor is nice. They have a full basement too and a nice size backyard," I said.

"Wait Red got a new girlfriend, I'm surprised. How is she? I see Kelly and Ant is still together," Kayla said.

"Her name is Denise and she seem cool, but a little stuck up. We exchanged numbers and I told her to call me. I never really hung out with her as of yet. Girl, Ant proposed to Kelly on Christmas. She said yes. Kelly had a Christmas party, but she didn't invite me. Vell went and when he asked me was I going I told him that I wasn't invited. I really don't care to around Kelly. You know you can't say anything to her without her popping off," I said.

"Wow that's good for them. But yes Kelly swear she's tough. She and Ciara both think that anyone can't beat or top them. That's cool though because when I get out I'm

214

going to be on my shit baby. Smooth better be ready to spend some paper on me and our baby," Kayla said.

I gave Kayla a high five. "I know that shit right, boo. You better make his ass pay. You and your baby shouldn't want for shit. I was just telling Vell that I was ready to trade my car in and get a new one," I said.

"Speaking of Vell, what's going on with you and him?" Kayla asked.

"Girl, Vell and I are cool. I just have to watch his ass harder now. He getting more money and these hoes are falling out of the sky. Girl, just the other day when I was driving his car, this chick was following me. When she was finally able to get on the side of me she was smiling and said, "Hey Vell." I said, "Nope it's not Vell bitch!" and she pulled off. I see her pick up her phone. I know she was calling him," I said.

"Girl, I know you went off on Vell," Kayla said.

"I asked him who she was and he was acting like he didn't know who I was talking about. Plus, the big booty chick next door stay in his face. Every time he pull up at the house she always in his face smiling and shit," I said.

"Does she speak to you? Do she have a man?' Kayla asked.

"She speaks, but that don't mean shit. No she doesn't have a man and always in Vell's face," I said.

"Wow, you better watch her. Coming from a friend that is the side chick. You better watch her ass," Kayla said laughing.

"Girl, I will fuck Vell and that hoe ass up! I just refused to lose to a side chick. No offense Kayla, but I understand what you saying," I said.

"None taken, hun. I feel like I'm not Smooth's side chick. Technically, I was with him before Ciara. We stopped messing around and she was able to slide in. Smooth was never truly with just Ciara," Kayla said.

"You right we all could see that. With his daughter Erica and then your unborn child, we can see that it's more too it," I said.

216

"I need to let you know that Smooth's mother agreed to keep the baby. I hope that you're fine with that. Smooth and I felt that with your children and plus our baby that would be too much for you and Vell to handle," Kayla said.

"That's fine as long as I and Vell are still the godparents," I said.

"Yes you both are still the godparents," Kayla said.

"Cool. I can't believe that Smooth's mother is keeping the baby. She might tell Ciara," I said.

"Aaliyah, please her loyalty is to her son. I'm sure that she doesn't approve of it, but is willing to help Smooth out," Kayla said.

"Yes, that's true," I said.

"I'm not worried about Ciara finding out. I will cross that bridge when I get there," Kayla said, "Look me in my face, I ain't got any worries, boo. Ciara needs to be worried about me," Kayla said eating her chips.

Ciara

I had a very long work week and I decided to treat myself to a private spa day. I just wanted to be alone and unwind. I needed a damn break from the children, Smooth, and every damn body. I told Smooth to hold the fort down for today. It was a cold Saturday afternoon thirty degrees to be exact. I didn't care I bundled up and hit the streets. There wasn't that much traffic out. I guess everyone was inside the house and snuggled up. Shit, I wasn't on none of that this year. Things just weren't the same. I wasn't in love with Smooth any longer. Everything that he did irked me. I couldn't stand when he touched me. Beside that, I'm still having those nightmares at night. I know that I said I would get help with my drinking this year, but I still haven't. I drink when I'm alone which is very rare, but when I do it just one glass only. Lately, I've been stressed out and unhappy. By looking at me you would never be able to tell. I hide it well so people will not see it. Those who are close to me can tell that I'm going through some thing, but they already know what's going on. Everyone knows that Smooth ain't shit and that I should just leave him alone. I'm at the point that I don't even argue with him, fuss, or fight. I'm just making it work for the children. Smooth is a good father; I will give him credit for that. I know that he's cheating again, but I really can't confirm it. I'm the type of woman who needs proof. It's killing me inside because Smooth is doing so good at hiding at. I'm always going through his things and I still end up finding nothing. I be so upset because I feel like he is winning and I'm losing. It's like we're playing games with one another and I'm tired of playing games. Last year, I accepted a lot of things because I was in love. Now, things have changed and I'm unhappy. It's hard to watch all my friends falling in love and be in happy relationships. Don't get me wrong, I'm happy for them, but I just wish that mine would work. I just want things back the way they used to be. My mind was spinning and I had to get a peace of mind. I made it to my destination, King Spa & Sauna. London told me about this place a while ago. I picked today to go. I walked in at immediately all my bad thoughts went away. I treated myself to a sixty minute deep massage. I choose a man to rub me down. It felt so good that I fell asleep. He tapped me when he was done. I made my way over to the sauna. It was my first time and the staff made me feel comfortable. I closed my eyes and relaxed. My mind started to think about Kanye. I never really stopped thinking about him since I got his number. London and I spoke of him and she said that he asks about me all the time. I felt good to know that someone was checking for me. I wanted to reach out to him, but I didn't want to seem too thirsty. What would I say? I haven't been with another man except for Smooth. I pushed my fear to the side and called him. His phone rang and on the fourth ring he answered.

"Hello," Kanye said.

I paused and didn't know what to say.

"Hello," Kanye said again.

"Hello, can I speak with Kanye?" I said.

"This is Kanye speaking," he said.

"Hello Kanye, this is Ciara, London's friend. Do you remember you and me meeting at her New Year's party?" I said.

"Yes, I remember you. I will never forget a beautiful woman such as yourself. How are you? I've been

220

waiting on your call. I've been asking London about you," Kanye said.

"I'm doing fine. How are you doing? Yes, London has been telling me that you have asked about me. I must admit that you have crossed my mind and that I've been meaning to call you," I said.

"I'm doing great now that you've called. What are you doing now? Are you free to meet me?" Kanye asked.

"I'm actually sitting in a sauna talking to you. I'm at Kings Spa & Sauna in Niles. After this, I will be free to meet you if that's fine with you," I said.

"Yes, it's fine to meet after. Do you mind meeting me at Cooper's Hawks in Arlington Heights?" Kanye asked.

"Yes, I would meet there. Can you give me an hour and I will see you then," I said.

"Fine, I will see you then beautiful, good bye," Kanye said.

I hung up the phone and smiled. I couldn't believe that I just called another man and accepted a date. I was curious to find out about Kanye. I needed some type of attention at the moment since Smooth was giving me the wrong type of attention. It was time for me to get back out here. I was much too young and beautiful to be miserable and unhappy. Besides, if Smooth can see other women, I feel as though I could see other men. I just hope that Kanye is single and don't have no drama. I already have my hands full with that. I have no more room for drama and pain. I allowed myself to soak and enjoy the sauna for twenty more minutes before I left. I dressed and bundled up and I prayed that I don't catch a cold. I'm happy that I did leave the house dressed properly for a date. I had on a black cashmere sweater, my high waist jeans, and my thigh high black boots on. My hair was softly curled. I made it to Coopers Hawk and called Kanye before I went inside. He was already there sitting at the table and waiting for me to arrive. I walked inside and I didn't care if I ran into anyone that I knew. I walked in like I was a single woman. I told the hostess that I was here with Kanye and she walked me to his table. Kanye stood as I approached him.

"Hello Ciara. You're looking beautiful as usual," Kanye said.

He pulled out my chair. I sat down and crossed my legs.

"Hello Kanye. Thank you for inviting me out to eat," I said.

"Wow, I didn't believe that you were actually going to call me. I've been thinking about you ever since the day that we met. I looked you up on the internet and checked out your business also. I see that you are about business and that's great," Kanye said.

"Wow, I see someone has been doing a background check on me." I blushed.

"I hope that I'm not coming off as a stalker. I like to check into people and things that I'm interested in," Kanye said.

"I'm actually flattered. I've never had anyone that I've known of check into me. Since you know what I do Mr., can you tell me what it is that you do?" I said.

"I'm an Architect. I'm twenty six years old, no children, and single," Kanye said.

"No crazy ex-girlfriends? Or women period who think that you two are involved?" I asked.

"None. I'm very single, never been married. I don't have any baggage, none whatsoever. I do recall you mentioning that you weren't single when you and I met. Has things changed?" Kanye said.

"As a matter of fact, things haven't change. It's leading towards that direction. I'm twenty four with two children, a stepmom to one. I was almost a wife last year until tragedy struck during my wedding ceremony. We didn't get married and ever since that day everything has pretty much gone downhill from there," I said.

The waitress politely interrupted us and asked if we were ready to order. We both were ready and Kanye allowed me to order first.

"May I have a bowl of your Tortilla Soup, the Spanish Seafood Cannelloni, and a glass of Sweet Wine," I said.

"Sir, what would you be having?" asked the waitress.

"I'm having Churrasco Grilled Steak with a side of Wasabi Buttered Potatoes, and a glass of Merlot," Kanye said.

The waitress left after we placed our orders. We resumed our conversation.

"I take it that you're unhappy," Kanye said.

"Yes I am. If I was happy, I wouldn't be here with you. I would not have taken your number at all," I said being honest.

"Well, I'm happy that I met you doing this stage in your life. Is there any hope in repairing your relationship?" Kanye asked.

"As of right now, I feel that's it over with. The only reason while it lasted this long was because of the children," I said.

"I see what you mean. How are your children doing the situation?" Kanye asked.

"The children are fine. My step daughter is three and my son is two. They're not aware of things going on. I try to get matters behind closed doors. They both spend a lot of times with their grandparents. I stay strong and keep a smile on my face for them. I and my man have been together for five years, but it seems like forever. He cheated on me, had a child on me, and that child's mother was tragically shot in front of her daughter during my wedding. I hope that sums it all up for you," I said.

The waitress bought our food and placed it front of us. I sipped on my glass of wine as Kanye sat back and watched me. He had a look on him that said, 'Wow!' I didn't mean to drop it on him like that, but I had to tell him. I was getting tired of telling the story, but I wasn't going to lie or sugarcoat shit. I hope I don't run his ass off because I'm curious to see what he's about. He gently grabbed my right hand.

"Ciara, I'm here for you and just the man you need to make all your pain go away. I don't care about him or how he fucked up. If you give me a chance, I promise not to ever hurt you. Despite the situation that you're in, I'm willing to overlook it and see what you're about," Kanye said.

"That's fine with me," I said.

Meanwhile back at home

Smooth

I had just ended my Saturday phone call with Kayla. She called at the right time. Ciara went to go do whatever the hell she was doing at left me with the children. This has started to become a routine thing so I just send them over to my mother house and let them spend time with her. I wasn't going to be in the house every Saturday with the children. Hell, I had moves to make. I got up with Vell. He told me to meet him at Hilton Express in Hillside. He owed me some money. When I pulled into the lot, I parked next to his car. I called and told him that I was downstairs waiting. He told me that he was about to send a girl down with my money. I said cool and waiting. A brown skinned, thick, big booty girl came walking through the doors. I honked the horn so that she could see me. She handed me the money and walked off. I looked at her walk away with all that ass. I called Vell.

"Who the fuck is that bro? She got hella ass. Damn, where you meet her at?" I asked.

"That's my side piece, Victoria. I didn't have to go far to meet her. She's my next door neighbor," Vell said.

"Damn bro, I thought I was foul, but you in first place for that move. Next door, how the hell you pull that off?" I asked.

"Aye, I will holler at you about it later. She's about to walk in," Vell said.

"Cool bro and make sure you wear a condom," I said.

"All the time, one," Vell said and hung up.

I hit 290 east and headed to the city. I called Ant and he said that he was out west at the spot. I exited off Austin and hit it down the street. Once I got to Augusta, I pulled into a park and went inside. Ant and a few of the shorties that worked with us was inside playing the game for money. They were playing Watch Dogs on Xbox. Ant was talking shit as usual.

"Hey you wanna play? Let me take you money, grab a remote," Ant said.

"Man nigga I don't play that shit," I said.

I went over to the workers and collected my money and counted it. I walked through the three bedroom apartment to check to see if everything was cool. I had to grab another stash house. I opened this one since I owned the building. It was a two flat brownstone and it had basement as well. I had tenants on the first floor and we occupied the second floor. I didn't allow no reckless shit to go on that could cause people to notice us. The shorties that I had staying there were of age and kept everything going. I went in one bedroom and to count the money to make sure everything added up. I looked at my phone to see what time it was and it was going on five p.m. 'What the fuck Ciara's ass doing,' I said to myself. I called her and she didn't pick up her phone. I called her ass again and she still didn't answer. I sent her a text asking where she was at. She didn't respond back. I went in the living room to join my peoples. We ordered pizza and wings. The food got here thirty minutes later. We ate and talked shit, my phone rang and it was Ciara.

"Aye, where you ass at Ciara and why you ain't answering the phone shit?" I said.

"I'm at home now and you didn't call my phone. What are you talking about, Smooth?" Ciara said.

"Don't play with me I called and texted your ass Ciara. Where the hell you been all day?" I said.

"I've been out. Where the fuck are you, Smooth?" Ciara said.

"I'm chilling and I will be home in a minute. Ciara be your ass in the house once I get there," I said.

"Smooth where the kids at?" Ciara asked.

"They at my mommy house. She will bring them back home tomorrow when she get out church," I said.

"Okay bye." Ciara said.

I hung up and ate my food. Ant and I started talking about booking our flights to the All-Star Game for next month. It was going to be in Dallas this year. You damn well we were going down there Tommy. That was the perfect time for me to go and handle business too. We were bringing our girls even though it was going to be a lot of pussy down there. Ciara wasn't going to let me go without her anyway. I smoked on a blunt and watched Ant lose on the game. That nigga is forever gambling. I told them to put in NBA 2k15, so that I can bust they ass and take all their money.

Ciara

I don't know why Smooth always took the children to his mom's house. My reason for leaving him with the kids was so he could spend some daddy time with them. Smooth sent them to his moms out of spite. The level that he's on he doesn't have to be out there. When he gets home, we are going to have a talk. I didn't feel like going there when I called him. I was still on cloud nine from my date that I was on with Kanye. I really enjoyed the food and had a great time and didn't want it to end. We talked about everything and I was happy that I could keep it real with him about my situation. He seemed mature and respectful. He wasn't a man that was in the streets. Kanye had a real career and made legit money. When he mentioned that he was working on the layout for Marino's and Tony's grocery store, I was impressed. He told me that he also designed his parent's home in Arizona that he had built from the ground. Kanye was the right type of man that I needed in my life. When I look back, I see how far that I have come. I give myself credit for that. I have grown in every aspect in my life. Smooth has remained in the same place and hasn't grown a bit. I was ready to grow and be happy, to travel and talk about mature things. To love all over again and not worry about my man fucking everything that looked good. I wanted my son to see a real father figure. Right now, he doesn't understand what is going on, but once he's older he's going to start asking questions. What would I tell him once he asks me what his father does for a living? Plus, I didn't want him to be affect by anymore of Smooth's foolishness. Bad enough Erica only has him to depend on as a biological parent. Her mom parents haven't even called or checked in on her. That bothers her because she asks about them all the time. I was ready for my breakthrough and I was going to get through all this bullshit at the end. I turned on some music and listen to Maxwell. I was thinking about Kanye and me as I listened to the words of Fortunate. My phone rang and interrupted me. It was Denise calling.

"Hey girl what's up?" I said.

"Hey Ciara. Are you free to talk?" Denise asked.

"Yes I am. What's up, is everything cool?" I asked.

"Oh yes everything is fine. I was calling to invite you to my Fellatio/Toy Party that I'm having the weekend before Valentine's Day," Denise said.

"That's going to be fun. I will be there hunny! I've never been to a Fellatio Party before. I heard they were a lot of fun. A girl could also use some toys," I said.

"Yes, we are going to have a lot of fun. I thought it would be great to get the ladies together. It's only going to be a small group because you know I really don't have many friends," Denise said.

"That's fine, hun just make that you don't forget to invite Kelly," I said.

"Oh I'm about to call her next. Make sure you save the date Ciara. I hope to see you there," Denise said.

"Okay, I will be there Neicy, ttyl," I said.

"Toodles hun!" Denise said.

I ended the call and went back to listening to Maxwell. The song Pretty Wings was now playing. I started thinking about Kanye again. I couldn't wait for the chance to be around him again. It's been a long time since I've been in the presence of a real man. I grabbed my laptop and googled his name, Kanye Freeman. His named popped up and so did a few articles who mentioned him. He was an Architect and was currently working on the new chain of grocery stores. I clicked on the pictures option and I see various pics of him with his business suits on. Damn, he looked fine; he favored the rapper Nelly, but was little taller. I read a few more articles on him and I was happy that he didn't lie about his career. I just hope that the rest was real and that he's really single. I wonder why he was available. I hope that he wasn't on the down low, you just never know. I wanted to call London and tell her all about my day, but I think that she might be with Jay. I will just wait until I see her on Monday and share everything with her. I know when I tell Kelly she is going to love the fact that I called him. Kelly has been telling me to get me to get me something on the side for the longest. I googled the salaries for Architects. Kanye said that he was a Consultant so that would make him an Architect V. Wow, they made almost $80,000 a year. That was nice, real nice. My phone rang and I see that it was Kanye calling. I answered the phone with my sexy voice.

"Hello Mr.," I said.

"Hello beautiful, I was calling to check on you to see that you were fine and made it home safely," Kanye said.

"That's nice of you to check up on me. It's very funny because I was just thinking about you," I said.

"Oh yeah, what were you thinking about?" Kanye asked.

"How I didn't want our date to end. I enjoyed myself and had a really good time. I can't wait to see you again," I said.

"I can't wait to see you again beautiful. I really enjoyed myself as well. You have such a wonderful personality. I like how laid back you are and don't let weigh you down. We have to set up something again really soon," Kanye said.

"Thank you I try to keep a smile on my face. I agree we have to see each other again. Our date went so fast," I said.

"Yes, I feel like I cheated you, but it was short notice. I have to plan something great next time. I'm quite sure I could come up with something special," Kanye said.

I listened to Kanye talk and my other line clicked. It was Smooth calling me. I let the other line click and continued my conversation. It was too good to end and besides I will see Smooth when he gets home. I listened Kanye tell me jokes and laughed. He had a good sense of humor.

"Ciara, you have a silly laugh," Kanye said.

"I know I was always told that. I'm silly and I love to laugh. I haven't had anyone make me laugh in a very long time," I said.

"Well, I'm the guy to change that. Don't worry I will keep you laughing and smiling. I can watch you smile all day," Kanye said.

"I'm looking forward to it," I said.

Kanye continued to talk and I heard Smooth pull into the garage. I didn't want to end to end the conversation, but I had to. I politely interrupted him and told him that I had to go and that I will call him tomorrow. We both said our goodbyes. I turned the music up louder. Smooth walked inside and I looked at him like I was shocked to see that he was home.

"Hey bae. I didn't even hear you come in," I said.

"Maybe because you had the music too loud. I called your phone several times, Ciara. Why didn't you answer the phone?" Smooth said.

"Really, did you? Maybe I didn't hear it because of the music," I said turning down the music.

"How was your day today? Did you enjoy yourself?" Smooth asked.

"My day was fine and yes I enjoyed myself," I said with a smile on my face.

Chapter Seventeen

Denise

I was calling and inviting people personally to my Fellatio/Toy Party that I was having next month. So far I've called and invited three of my closest girlfriends from school, two of my cousins, and Ciara and Kelly. The last person to call on the list was Aaliyah. I really didn't know her, but we did exchange numbers at Ciara's place back in November. She seemed cool and since she was Vell's girl I decided to invite her. I dialed her number and she answered.

"Hello, can I speak with Aaliyah?" I asked.

"This is Aaliyah speaking, may I ask who's calling?" Aaliyah said.

"Hey Aaliyah, this is Denise, Red's girlfriend," I said.

"Oh hey Denise, how are you? Girl, I didn't know who you were," Aaliyah said laughing.

"I know I can tell by the tone of your voice that you're wondering who was calling. Anyway, I'm doing fine girl. I called to invite you to my Fellatio/Toy Party that I'm having next month. I plan to have it the weekend before Valentine's Day. I would love if you could make," I said.

"Count me in. It sounds like fun. I love doing things like that. Is there going to be a lot of people? Who all did you invite? Do you need any help?" Aaliyah asked.

"It's only going to be maybe ten of us. Its invite only because I don't really feel comfortable with people I don't know in my home. The only people that you know who I invited are Ciara and Kelly. As of now, I don't need any help. I will keep you in mind if I do," I said.

"Okay just let me know if you need help. I totally understand about having strangers in your home. I'm really happy that you invited me. I will be there," Aaliyah said.

"Great, I can't wait to finally hang out with you and get a chance to know you," I said.

"Yes Denise the feeling is mutual. I will save your number in my phone," Aaliyah said.

"Cool, I'm going to text you the invitation and my address will be on there. Hope to see you soon. Toodles," I said.

"Goodbye," Aaliyah said.

Okay so that's everyone. I was done inviting everyone and a week prior to the event I will send out text messages. I had a funny feeling about Aaliyah. I mean so far she was cool. What concerned me was when she asked who I invited. I felt like she was setting me up with that question. At Ciara's Thanksgiving dinner, I noticed that she was quiet and pretty much to herself. She and Ciara said very little to one another. I think that Ciara only deals with her on the strength of Smooth and Vell's friendship. Aaliyah didn't come to Kelly's Christmas dinner. I noticed that Aaliyah and Kelly didn't speak to one another while at Ciara's place. Kelly is the type of person who keeps it real and don't sugar coat shit. I liked that. Ciara and Kelly were both cool and fun to around. I didn't have a problem with them. I want to ask them about Aaliyah, but first I want to get to know her myself. When it came to her, I couldn't read her. I'm usually good at reading people too. I guess I will find out and see what she is like when she comes to my party. I just hope that she doesn't keep up bullshit and start a lot of shit. I have no more room for drama in my life. I have a small circle and I like it that way. Even though my circle is small, I still have to watch them as well. I pretty much never got along with females and just clicked with my cousins. Girls never really liked me they think that I'm stuck up. Really, I'm not I just prefer nice things. I grew up being the only child. My parents didn't have much, but they made sure that I had what I needed. I went to Malcolm X College and got my Associate of Arts in Teaching-Early Childhood Education. While I was going to school, I worked for Edna's Daycare. Edna was an older lady who owned her own at home daycare and stayed down the street from me. I started working for her when I turned eighteen years old. Working for her and around children lead me to want to go to school for it. When people asked what I was majoring in and I told them they would ask me do I like working around children. I tell them I love working with children. Another reason why I loved working with children was because I don't think that I can have them. I've been pregnant twice in the passed and I lost them because I couldn't carry children. So being around other people children fills that void in my life. I want children and Red and I have talked about it as well. Red doesn't have any children either, but he's fine with the fact that I can't carry. He says don't worry about it and one day we will both have our child. I loved Red and I accept him and his past. I met Red while I was walking downtown. I was shopping on State Street and he was riding down State and let down his window to flirt with me.

"Excuse me beautiful. I'm lost can you tell me how to get to LaSalle?" he asked.

"Sure, you just keep street and should just run into it. It's three blocks down," I said.

"Thank you, but before I pull off can I get to know you?" he asked.

I looked at him like he was crazy. The light turned green and cars were blowing their horn. It he didn't move his car and remained there.

"My name is Red, what's your name?" he asked.

"You better drive, you're holding up traffic," I said.

243

"I'm not pulling off until I get your name and number," he said.

"I gave him my name and number as cars drove past him and drivers cursing him out. By that time the light had changed and that's when he asked me to get inside the car with him. I looked at his ass like he was crazy.

"Hey, why don't you get inside with me and we can go and have some lunch," he said.

"First of all, I don't know you. Second, I have my own car. Third, the answer is no," I said.

"Ok I see that you're the sassy type. Check it out, I will call you tonight, Neicy," he said and drove off.

I know I could've sent him off and gave him the wrong number, but I was curious to find out who he was. Late that night, Red called me and he was still trying to see me.

"So Neicy what are you doing now? Do you want to come outside with me tonight?" Red asked

"Go outside where this late Red?" I asked it was going on nine pm.

"We can go to the strip club, KOD," Red said.

"I don't know I've never been to the KOD before. I heard it was kind of ratchet," I said.

"KOD is cool. Come out with me you will be fine," Red said.

"I guess I will go, but I'm driving my own car," I said.

"That's cool baby girl. Meet me on Augusta and Austin when you're ready," Red said.

I put on a little dress and some heels and headed out the door. I've never been to a strip club before so I hope it would be fine. I pulled up on Austin and Augusta and called Red. He came down and begged me to get in the car with him.

"You should leave your car parked and jump in with me," Red said.

"I'm not leaving my car over here," I said.

"Please jump in the car with me. I promise you will be safe," Red said.

I jumped in the car with him and we rode to the strip club. Once we walked in KOD, there was a fight. I was so mad because I should've listened to myself and not come. This place was ratchet. Even the strippers looked basic. I cursed at myself for not driving my car instead. Red was having a good time and enjoying the ratchet crowd. Every stripper came up to him and was trying to do a lap dance for him. All the cars knew him. At the time I didn't know why, I found out later that Red had some money and a weakness for hoes. Thirty minutes another fight broke out and they shut the club down. I was so happy and ready to go. On the ride home, Red asked me to spend the night with him.

"Are you spending the night with me?" Red asked.

"Hell no. Are you serious? I don't know you. You can just take me to my car," I said.

"I'm sorry if I offended you. I'm just used to women giving me the pussy on the first night," Red said.

"Well, I don't get down like that. You shouldn't get down like that either. It's too much shit out here to be doing all that," I said.

Red turned up the music and hit the Dan Ryan Expressway. I sat back and enjoyed the ride to my car. I couldn't wait till I got home. We made it out west in twenty minutes due to him speeding. When I got to my car, I had a boot on it.

"Fuck! The boot man got me. I knew I should have drove my car. I don't have the money to get this boot off my car," I said.

"Chill, let's just see how much you owe and I will pay for it," Red said.

We went to go pay to get the boot off my car. I owed $2000 in parking tickets and plus I had to pay an additional $160 for the boot removal fee. Red paid for everything. By the time I got my car back, it was daylight. I went home with Red, but we didn't sleep together. He stopped me when I was trying to give him some.

"No Denise, you're not that type of girl," Red said.

247

"But, I want to thank you for getting my boot off my car," I said.

"No I'm straight. If I sleep with you right now, you'll never hear from me again. I like you Denise and want to get to know you. Besides, that was little money," Red said.

"Well, why am I here right now? If you don't want to sleep with me, you could've let me go home," I said.

"I just want to get to know you and I didn't want you to leave," Red said.

We stayed up all morning and talked getting to know one another. I told Red that I wanted my own a daycare one day. Red shared with me that he just wanted one girl and was ready to slow down. We both shared a lot that morning and eight months later we are still together. At first, our relationship was a mess. I had to deal with all of Red ex-girlfriends. They couldn't accept the fact that he had one girl and wasn't interested in dealing with them. After a while, things died down and we were fine. But, every once in a while I still might have to check a hoe or two. Red had a weakness for big asses. I didn't have a lot of ass so he convinced me into getting surgery. I agreed and got the surgery. I didn't have enough fat on my body to get transferred into my butt so I got butt implants. Red loved it. I getting butt implants was the talk of the town, but I didn't care. Red and I was in love and that was all that mattered.

Ebony

I completed my Pole Dancing Class 101 and now I was in Pole Dancing 201. I was still hanging in there. I was doing great and was able to climb the pole, but I couldn't get down the pole. I went to my classes and watched Tia work that pole. She was great at what she did, but that still didn't stop me from wanting to get to know her man. Last week he came up here to meet with her and she excused herself from the class. He looked good just like the girl told me and had a muscled body. I watched him, but he didn't even notice me. I noticed him though and I was plotting in my head how to get him. I snapped out of my trance thinking about Tia's man. I had to focus on learning how to work that pole so that I could start working. I wanted to still check out a few spots to see if they would still hire me. I would be a bartender or anything just to get my foot in the door. It was crunch time, meaning that my cash was getting low. I had to bust some moves around this bitch soon so that I don't hit rock bottom. It was our turn to use the pole and Tia was talking.

"Ok class I'm going to demonstrate the Cupid move for you. The first time I'm going to slow it down. Once I'm done, you will give it try," Tia said.

Tia worked the pole and gave the instructions.

"I'm going to start by working it from the floor so that you understand that it's really a push pull. Keep your hips as far from the pole as possible. The top knee is the pull. The bottom foot is providing the push. Let me show you from another angle. Notice my top knee is only about waist high. So, from a side climb keep your hips back as you hook the top leg. Hook at waist height and set your bottom foot with a bent knee and straighten to pop up. Grasp you shin and release the top hand, pushing your hips forward. To maintain the hold and stop from slipping, you can squeeze your top leg to the pole. The top knee should be keeping you from falling away from the pole. You are not hanging off it. The bottom foot should be pushing the pole away from you. Let me repeat it over, but I'm going to do it faster," Tia instructed.

Tia got on the pole and showed the class the Cupid move at a faster pace. I sat there and studied her. One by one, each of us demonstrated back to her. We all did great and I was starting to be able to climb up the pole. I made a few mistakes that Tia pointed out.

"Ebony you're setting your top knee too high. I want you to squeeze and stay active by using your inner thigh," Tia said.

"Okay like this?" I said demonstrating the move.

"Yes perfect, now come down, but try not to pull your weight out. That will cause your weight to drop straight down and your foot will slide," Tia said.

I did what Tia instructed me to do. I was actually waning down the pole with ease.

"Great job Ebony! Okay class next week I will be going over the Corkscrew Spin. For those of you who have a pole at home, I want you to practice doing the Cupid at home. Everyone did great and I will see you next week," Tia said.

I gathered my things and prepared to leave. I headed to go and sign up at the gym. Yes, I was joining Snap Fitness to in hopes of running into Tommy. I had my eye on his ass. I didn't give a fuck about Tia. I mean I respect her and give her props. I like her lifestyle and I want to live like that. Hell, I couldn't get that type of lifestyle in Chicago because I was pretty much known as a money hungry hoe. Which I am, buts what's wrong with a girl wanting a man with some bread? I had a chance to start all over down here and didn't anyone know me nor my background. I walked to the front desk of Snap Fitness.

"Hello, I'm interested in joining your gym," I said to the lady at the desk.

"Hello, welcome to Snap Fitness. I will be able to assist you with that," the lady said.

The lady went over the rates and gave me a tour of the gym. It was nice gym that offer many things. I didn't care about the amenities I just was here to run into Tommy. The good thing about the gym was that it was 24 hours. So I could come in here anytime to sweat it out. I paid for my 1 year membership. I went my ass home to my baby Kimora. Stella was there doing her same routine that was watching Lifetime. Baby Kimora was sleeping taking her nap. Stella left shortly. I kicked back and called my cousin Rio.

"Hey Rio, what's up?" I said.

"What's up Ebony? Shit, I'm riding and smoking now," Rio said.

"Did I call you at the wrong time? You need me to call you back?" I asked.

"Nawl, you cool cuz. I'm just busting some moves. How baby Kimora doing?" Rio asked.

"She cool. She's sleep right now. Cuz, so what's been going on in the Chi?" I said.

"Same ole shit just a different toilet. Aye, your boy Ant and Kelly getting married. Kelly riding around with a big rock on her finger," Rio said.

"What!! Are you fucking serious?! I hate that bitch, Kelly!" I said.

"Yeah, I heard he proposed to her on Christmas or some shit," Rio said.

"That bitch better be lucky that I'm not still in Chicago. I will make her life a living hell. I fucking hate Kelly. I knew Ant was going to marry her ass. He just using that girl because she going to college and shit. Niggas always making them type their wifey's, but be doing the most out in the streets," I said.

"Oh I forgot, she was going to Chicago State," Rio said.

"The bitch should be graduating this year. She majoring in Business/Finance I believe," I said.

"Hold Ebony, I got another call," Rio said.

I waited on hold. Damn the shit I just heard really hit me hard. I'm not going to lie. I'm mad as fuck that bitch Kelly is getting married to Ant. Even though I could never be back with him, I didn't want Kelly to be with him. I hated her and the reason why was because I really loved Ant. He was my first love and I did everything he asked me to do in the bedroom. I now wish we were back the way

254

they used to be before Rich kidnapped him. I might have still had a chance even though Kimora wasn't his baby. I know for a fact if I was still living in Chicago that I would be still be fucking him. Rio clicked back over.

"My fault cuz, that was this little bitch that I'm about to scoop up. What were we talking about again?" Rio said.

"I was talking about Ant and Kelly, but fuck them. I hope they both get hit by a truck," I said.

"Cuz your ass crazy. Fuck them though. Live your life down there in Texas and get your shit together. There's no need to hate on them. You cool ain't shit happening in Chicago," Rio said.

"You're right about me getting my shit together. But, I'm not hating on them! I just fucking hate Kelly," I said.

"Fuck that shit! Have you got in touch with your mom down there yet?" Rio said.

"No I haven't," I said.

"Ebony, why haven't you called your mom? You need to get in contact with her," Rio said.

"Why should I get in contact with her? Rio, she left me and said fuck me. So I feel the same way about her," I said.

"Ebony, you need to reach out to your mom. You living off the past and what your father was telling you. Maybe you need to hear her side of the story," Rio said.

"I don't know Rio. I'm just so angry with her. At this point, I went this long without her in my life why do I need her now?!" I said.

"Fuck it Ebony! If you want to act childish, then that's your business. You need to reach out to your mom. Hell, you already lost your father," Rio said.

"Whatever Rio! I'm hanging up now before I say something I regret," I said.

"Cool cuz, I will holler at you later." Click. Rio hung up.

I didn't care about him hanging up on me. I mean damn if I didn't feel like calling my mother then let it be. That was something that I didn't want to do. I was angry that she left and choose a man over her family. What type of mother does that?! I could care less what Rio is talking about. I was angry with my mom and I hated her too. As a matter of fact, fuck everyone. I'm all about me and Kimora. If my mother wanted to reach out to me, she knew where to find me. I don't care that she lives down here with her second husband. Yes, second fucking husband. She still didn't come back to check on me after losing her first husband. I blame her for the way that I turned out. Maybe if I had a mother to teach me how to be a lady, I wouldn't be such a hoe. I didn't have a role model. My father told me to keep my legs closed, but he couldn't really teach me how to be a lady. He was there every time I fucked up to bail me out. He couldn't wait when I was old enough to move out and get my own place. The women that I learned from were the ones I was surrounded by and the ones I seen on television. All of them were about one thing and that was getting money. I didn't have a mom to encourage me to stay in school. It's fucked that I don't even have a high school diploma. Hell, I didn't have a mother to teach me how to cook, do hair, nothing. I learned those things from Shunda's mother. That's why I was always with her and at her home spending the nights. Shunda's mother was like a mother to me, but she wasn't the perfect mom. She was one of those get money, fuck niggas type moms, but at least she was there for Shunda. I wasn't ready to face my mother if I see her right now I might smack her ass. I had other shit to be worried about like trying to get up with Tia's man Tommy. All-Star Weekend was coming up next month and I had to be prepared. It was going to be a lot of money out here and I had to ready to make it.

Chapter Eighteen

February arrived and winter came along. I was busy at Bella's ordering new items for the boutique. It was snowing out and starting to stick. I didn't have a customer walk in yet. London wasn't scheduled to come in for another hour. I was thinking about calling her and telling her that she didn't have to come in. The snow was falling heavier and I believe that I'm going to close early. I turned on the television to watch the news. On every news station, they were reporting the weather. A snow storm was on the way. Okay, I'm going to close early for today. I was about to call London, but the shop phone rang.

"Hello Bella Boutique," I said.

"Hey Ciara, it's me London. How is everything going up at the shop?" London asked.

"Hey London, I was just about to call you. It's pretty slow. I think that I'm about to close early," I said.

"Yes, it's bad out there. That's why I called first to check in," London said.

"Well hun just take the day off. I'm closing and heading home. I don't want to be out here in this mess," I said.

"Okay, I will see you tomorrow, but I will call you first before I come. You be careful getting home Ciara," London said.

"Okay and enjoy your day off. Goodbye," I said ending the call.

The news reporter was standing outside in Wheaton giving the weather. She had on her coat, hats, and gloves. The wind was blowing her around and the snow was falling really heavy.

"Good afternoon, I'm reporting live from Wheaton, Illinois and as you can see the wind is really furious out here. The snow is falling and we are expecting between 10' to 15' inches of snow. The national forecast center says that a snow storm is on the way. The snow will be getting heavier throughout the day. By the evening, we could see at least 13' inches." The news reporter said.

The reporter fell to the ground, but continued to tell the news. I laughed at her because she was crazy for going out there in the first place. I went to the door to lock it. I started my car up so that it can warm up. I closed the blinds and went back to cleaning up a few things before I headed out. I had to go to the grocery store to get some food. I didn't want to be stuck in the house during a snow storm without any food. Damn! The children I have to pick them up too. Maybe Smooth could get them instead. I called Smooth.

"Hey bae you think you can go pick the children up now? The snow is really coming down bad and I don't want to be out there this evening picking them up," I said.

"Yes, I will pick them up. How are you up at the boutique? Are you leaving and coming home?" Smooth asked.

"Yes, I'm about to close early. I have to go to the grocery store to pick up some food. I'm stopping off at Food   4 Less before I come home," I said.

"Cool, I will go and get the children now. Call me if you need me baby," Smooth said.

"Okay, I will call you, but I'm sure that I will be fine. Good bye talk to you soon," I said.

I went to log on to Instagram and Facebook to tell my customers that I was closed for the rest of the day due to the snow storm. I logged off and wrapped up and stepped outside. My car was ready and I hopped in. I drove down Harlem and people were acting like they couldn't drive with the little snow on the ground. I blew my horn because they were acting like it was the first time that it snowed in Chicago. I made it to Food 4 Less and it was swamped with people. I did my grocery shopping making sure I had meat, sides, and plenty of junk food. I grabbed me a bottle of wine too. Smooth called to check on me and I told him that I was fine. I went to stand in line and of course it was only two lines open. You know I said something because I wasn't about to stand in a long ass line. I went to speak to a manager and they opened another line. When the cashier announced that another line was open, everyone tried to run over there. I went off.

"Excuse me, but I'm going ahead of all you," I said pushing my cart toward the front of the line. I placed my food on the belt. This younger girl and her crew had the nerve to get mad.

"Who does she think she is? Miss America or somebody?" one girl said.

I ignored the young girl because she didn't know any better. She could not have known any better fucking with me. I put my food on the belt one by one. She was still talking shit in the background, but I ignored her and bagged my food as the cashier rang me up. I put my bags in the cart and went back to pay for my food. I was standing at the register and pulled my card out to pay. The young girl was placing her food on the belt and she bumped me purposely. I turned around and smacked that bitch. SMACK! Everyone looked in shocked. The young girl tried to hit me in my face with a box of Cap 'n' Crunch. Her friends tried to jump me. I hit another girl and to get her ass out the way until I grabbed my purse. They fucked up now. I went in my purse and pulled out my gun.

"She got a gun!" one girl yelled.

"Run up now! I will shoot all you bitches!" I yelled.

Everyone screamed and got low on the floor. I wasn't trying to shoot anyone, but them bitches wasn't about to jump on me. I put my gun back in my purse and pushed my cart of food out the door. Everyone just watched me walk out the door. Melrose Park police came in while I was walking out. The manager was explaining to them what happened. I was putting my groceries in the car when they approached me outside. The crew of girls were following behind them and pointing at me.

"That's her right there officers. She's the one who pulled out a gun on me," the young girl said.

"Miss we received a phone call stating that a woman who fits your description pulled out a firearm inside Food 4 Less," the fat officer said.

"Yes I did, but I have my registration to carry a firearm," I said pulling it out of my purse.

The officer looked at it and then he asked could he see my driver's license. I didn't mind so I gave it to him as well. The officer ran my name as I sat inside my car. He walked back to the car and gave me back my license.

"Here is your documents back Ms. Robinson. You are free to go," the officer said.

"Hell nawl, you are going to let her go after she pulled a gun out on me!" the young girl said.

"Ma'am calm down before I have to arrest you," the officer said to the young girl.

"Fuck keeping calm! That bitch pulled a gun out on us and you letting her go!" she said.

I pulled off and waved goodbye to her and her ratchet crew.

Fellatio/Toy Party

Denise

Everyone gathered in my apartment in Oak Park for my Fellatio/Toy party. I had appetizers and drinks. My cute party favors were fun and flirty. I had a cake in the shape of a black penis. The girls thought it was cute. I introduced everyone so that people wouldn't be looking silly at each other. A few people have already met Ciara before from shopping at Bella Boutique. Kelly and my cousin was busy talking about something. I don't know as long as everyone was enjoying themselves. Aaliyah was pretty much off to herself so I went to go over and talk to her.

"Hey Aaliyah are you enjoying yourself? By the way, I love your boots, they're very nice. Where did you get them?" I asked.

"Hey Neicy and yes I am enjoying myself. I'm just sitting back and chilling. Thank you I got my boot from DSW," Aaliyah said.

"Okay well, you can move around and mingle. You don't have to be over her in the corner all by yourself," I said.

"I spoke to everyone earlier. I'm just sitting here and waiting for the lady to arrive," Aaliyah said sipping on her drink.

"She should be here any minute now. I just want to make sure that you're enjoying yourself," I said.

I walked away and went to the back to get more liquor for the girls. Kelly walked back there.

"Hey Neicy don't pay Aaliyah any mind. I overheard you talking to her. Look, let me share something with you. Ciara and I beat her cousin's ass years ago and Aaliyah really doesn't care for us. So if you wondering why we not cool with her that is the reason why. I don't fuck with her period, but Ciara talks to her at times. But, I don't want you to stop being friends with her. You have every right to be friends with whoever, but just don't tell her your business. She's not to be trusted," Kelly said.

"Girl, I was wondering why you all were so distanced with one another. I could tell that something had gone on. Thanks for the heads up because I don't know her, but I felt since she was Vell's girl then I would invite her too," I said.

"That's fine and Ciara feels that way as well, but I don't. Ant and Vell understands so I don't be bothered with her. Because the way I'm sat up, if she say anything to me wrong I will beat her ass. So to keep the peace I keep my

267

distance. So let her sit right there all night so no bullshit won't be started," Kelly said.

"Okay Kelly because I don't want no fighting inside my house," I said.

"Oh I will never do that. I will respect your place hun," Kelly said.

I grabbed a few more bottles and took them in the front. Kelly carried the bucket of ice.

"More drinks ladies! Who wants Remy?" I asked.

"I will take a glass," Ciara said.

I poured Ciara a glass of Remy. Everyone asked for different drinks and I served them. The lady Angela showed up to teach her fellatio class. She passed out dildos and condoms. Everyone laughed as we passed around the dildos. Our first lesson was putting the condom on with our mouth. Angela demonstrated the skill once she was done it was our turn. I put my own with a problem. Some of the girls had a problem. The next thing she showed us was how to lick a man's balls. Now, that was hilarious. You should have seen us licking on the dildo balls. The next trick she went over was learning how to deep throat. She told us that gagging was good and that men loved when a woman gagged on his penis. The more salvia the better the performance. We had to put the dildo in our mouth as far as we could go. It was fine if we gagged, but we had to relax. Angela walked to each girl one by one to make sure that we were doing it right. When she got to me, she laughed and said, "I see we have ourselves a pro here." I was embarrassed, but laughed it off. I know how to suck a dick, but I just wanted to get better. It was a lot of new tricks out here and I wanted to learn them all. Just to make sure Red doesn't have to depend on the next chick to suck his dick. The last move that Angela showed us was how to suck your man penis from the back. Now, that was weird, but she said that had husband loved it. I think that I would pass on that move. At the end, Angela showed us how she sucks her husband by using the dildo. She was sucking, slurping, and gagging. It was messy and sloppy just like men liked it. Nasty and freaky was a better way to describe it. Everyone sat back and watched her and when she was done she asked if we had any questions.

"I have a question. Why do you have so much salvia coming from your mouth? I mean doesn't everything get wet?" I asked.

"Yes, but the wetter the better. When the penis goes deeper in your mouth that's when your gag reflex starts to kick in. That is what produces the salvia," Angela said.

"How do you know if your man is enjoying it?" my cousin asked.

"You have to communicate with your partner. Talk nasty to him while you're sucking his cock. Trust me he will talk back and tell you what to do. He will also tell you if he likes it," Angela said.

"What should I do with my tongue while I am sucking his dick?" Aaliyah said.

"Great question. There are different variations of licking, softly, forcefully, using your full tongue. Try using the tip of your tongue, quick fluttering motions, long slow licks, or swirling your tongue around the head of his penis. It is really up to you and your lover to find out what he likes best. You can also lick him anywhere from his anus to the tip of his cock," Angela said.

"Gross!" Ciara said sipping on some Remy.

"I know a lot of women say that. The most important thing to do is keep your tongue pressed against the underside of his cock. As you move back and his cock comes out of your mouth, keep the tip of your tongue focused just under the tip, where the ridge comes up to meet the urethral hole. You can even flick this area as you slide your mouth up and down to further the effect. Doing that allows him to feel both the soft and the rough side of the tongue," Angela.

"Well I really learned a lot today. Now, let's pull out the toys," I said.

Angela placed her toys out on the table. She had all type of dildos. Everyone gathered around and picked the items that they wanted to buy. I bought some hand cuffs, a silver bullet, and some oral sex numb mints. Ciara bought a sex game and some handcuffs. Kelly bought some good head for oral sex. Aaliyah bought a vibrating tongue ring that you put around your tongue. She also bought the rabbit.

271

I whispered to Angela and told her to put me an amazing fellatio kit to the side. Hey I didn't want everyone in my business I'm just saying. Everyone gathered their things and prepared to leave.

"Thank you all for coming out and having a good time," I said giving all my guest a hug before they left.

"Thank you for inviting us, hun. Next weekend is Valentine's Day. Oh, are you going to the All-Star Game?" Ciara asked me.

"Hell yes. I'm not letting Red go down there and leave me here," I said.

"I know that shit right, boo! Well, I will see you then. I will call you, Neicy," Ciara said.

"Thanks Neicy, I had a lot of fun and I will see you two in Texas," Kelly said giving me a hug.

"Bye Kelly and Ciara," I said.

"Thanks for inviting me, Neicy. We have to hang out again just you and me," Aaliyah said.

"That's cool just let me know. Maybe we can go shopping or out to eat one day," I said.

"Yes girl. Okay ttyl," Aaliyah said leaving.

Eventually, everyone was gone. I called Red as I was cleaning up and told him to come on over. I wanted to try some of my tricks that I learned on him.

Valentine's Day

Ciara

Valentines fell on a Thursday this year. Bella Boutique has been busy all week. Today was no different and London and I didn't even get a chance to take a break. Women were busy buying something to wear for their significant other. Another reason why I was so busy was that it was also All-Star Weekend. The entire city of Chicago was going to be down in Texas. Item after item has been flying off the racks. I was used to being busy all the time, but this was quite overwhelming. The phones were ringing off the hook and it got to the point that I wasn't answering them any longer. I thought the weather outside was going to slow people down. It was 20 degrees and freezing outside. The snow had finally given us a break, but the cold didn't. Around 1p.m. it slowed down a bit. London and I ordered from Jimmy Johns for delivery. We really didn't feel like going out in the cold to get lunch. Twenty minutes later our sandwiches arrived and we sat down and ate.

"Ciara, what do you and Smooth have planned for Valentine's?" London asked.

"Smooth and I are staying in this year. We are sending the children to their grandmas until Monday until we return from Texas. Thank you again for running the boutique for me the next four days. I hope it's not too much trouble," I said.

"Oh no, I will be fine. Don't worry, I can hold down the fort," London said.

"What are you two love birds doing? I know Jay has something romantic planned," I said.

"We are going to the Signature Room. I'm so excited I've never been before," London said.

"It's a lovely place. The food is delicious. You two are going to enjoy it," I said.

London and I continued to talk about tonight's plans. The door swung open and a man came inside carrying a box and some roses.

"Excuse me ladies, I am looking for Ciara," the man said.

"I'm Ciara," I said.

"Well, this is for you," the man said giving me the two items.

I took the box and the roses. The box had a card attached to it. London read the card for me like she usually did.

"Roses are red. Violets are blue. Take a chance at life. You'll find the new you. From Kanye," London read.

London and my mouth dropped. I just knew that Smooth had sent me these gifts.

"Girl, open up the box. I wanna see what's inside," London said.

I unwrapped the box. You could tell by the style of the box that it was a pair of shoes. I opened up the box and it was a pair of the So Kate Booty by Christian Louboutin.

"Wow, I can't believe that he got these. How did he get them?! These just came out online and were out of stock in twenty minutes," I said surprised.

"Girl, these boots are so cute," London said holding one in her hand.

"I have to call him. Excuse me, London, I'm going to my office to make a private call," I said.

"No problem girl. Gone and call your boyfriend," London teased me and said.

I went in my office and sat down to call Kanye on Skype. Before I called him, I made sure that I looked good. I applied more lip gloss and puckered my lips. I called and his face popped up on the screen after the first ring.

"Hello beautiful. I take it that you have received my gifts," Kanye said.

"Yes I did. The roses are lovely. The booties are so cute. Thank you Kanye, but you didn't have to buy me such an expensive gift," I said.

"You're welcome and you deserve it. You are exclusive Ciara. One of a kind," Kanye said.

"I miss you so much. How is work in California?" I asked.

"I miss you too my chocolate drop. Work is work. I wish that you were here with me," Kanye said.

"I wish I was as well. I can't wait till the 23rd gets here," I said.

"Maybe I could see you sooner than the 23rd. That's if you let me fly you in after you return from Texas," Kanye said.

"I will like that, but I don't know Kanye. He isn't letting me go out of town. And besides what reason will I use to go to California?" I said.

"Yeah you right. Damn Ciara, I miss you baby, but I have to end this call and get back to work. You have a wonderful day beautiful," Kanye said.

"I will call you this evening. You enjoy your day as well," I said.

Evening

Smooth and I were alone. The candle were lit and R. Kelly was playing in the background. I had on red lace cutout garter slip and ruby red lips. Smooth was enjoying the massage that I was giving him. I was lying on him and rubbing his back with baby oil. I know that Smooth and I have been arguing a lot lately. I calmed down a notch since I've been seeing Kanye on the side. I know that it was wrong, but when I was with Kanye it felt so right. Smooth has been doing pretty good lately so I decided to play nice and stopped all the arguing and fighting.

"You are so tense, Smooth. Are you enjoying the massage?" I asked.

"Yes Blackbone, you are doing such a wonderful job. I'm so stressed because it's a lot going on out here in the streets," Smooth said.

"Well, I want you to forget all about everything that is stressing you out. Think about things that make you happy," I said.

Smooth turned around on his back to face me. "I will think about you and our children. You are so beautiful, Blackbone. Guess what I have a surprised for you," Smooth said.

"You do? Where? Are you hiding it?" I asked Smooth.

"It's in the closet. On my side behind my clothes," Smooth said.

I ran to the closet and pulled out two boxes that were hidden behind Smooth's clothes on his side of the closet. It was a long box and a smaller box. I unwrapped them as Smooth watched me. Inside the longer box was a black mini sleeveless Versace. Inside the smaller box was a pair of So Kate Booty by Christian Louboutin. I played it off and looked surprised even though I received the same boots earlier from Kanye.

"The dress and boots are beautiful. Thank you Smooth!" I said giving him a hug.

"I was hoping that you will like the dress. I overheard you telling Kelly that you wanted the boots. So I went on and grabbed them," Smooth said.

"Thank you bae, I love you so much," I said wrapping my arms around him and giving him a kiss.

Smooth kissed me back and both our tongues danced. He slipped off my slip and laid me down kissing me deeply. He kissed the side of my neck hitting my spot making my clit moist. His tongue worked its way down to my breast. He sucked on both of my nipples one by one. I moaned lightly and watched him as he sucked on them like they were melons. I was getting too excited and wanted to feel him.

"Make love to me, Smooth," I whispered in his ear.

"I love you so much, Ciara," Smooth said.

He went inside of me and pumped vigorously. My breasts bounced from left to right. Smooth placed my legs on his shoulders and plunged in me deeper. I dug my nails in his back. He cupped my ass with both of his hands.

"Stop running. You gonna give my pussy," Smooth said.

"Ohhhhhh, Ohhhhhh, Smooth Yes! Yes!" I said.

"You gonna stop being stingy with my pussy?!" Smooth said pumping inside of me.

"Yesssssss, I'm gonna stop being stingy, daddy!" I moaned.

"Whose pussy is this?!" Smooth said.

"Your pussy, daddy!" I said.

"Damn, I'm about to bust baby. Ciara, I'm about to nut!" Smooth said.

He pulled out and shot his hot sticky sperm on my thigh.

All-Star Weekend

Kelly

It was All-Star Weekend baby and me and my girls were going with our men. We touched down in Houston, Texas baby and I was feeling this weather. We were staying at the Houston Marriott West Loop by the Galleria. I was so excited and ready to hit the Galleria Mall. Once Ant and I got to our room, we fell across the king sized bed.

"This is nice Ant. So what's the plan for today?" I asked.

"Shit me and the fellas about to meet up with Tommy and his people. So we can go handle some business. What you about to do?" Ant asked.

"You know me. I'm about to hit the mall. Me and girls, you know girly stuff," I said.

"Cool, you need some money? We might hit the mall once we finish taking care of business," Ant said.

"Okay well, I need at least $2500. I have some cash on me too. I just need to grab a few pieces," I said.

"You sure that's all you need? Here take $10,000 I know you and I know how you shop. Enjoy yourself babe. Tear the mall up, you outta town," Ant said.

"Thank you baby, I love you so much. I can't wait till we walk down the aisle," I said.

"I love you Kelly. You know you mean the world to me," Ant said kissing me.

I kissed him back as I unfasten his Gucci belt and unzipped his pants. Ant's dick was rock hard and heavy. It was only right if I sucked his dick. Besides, we was in Houston at the All-Star Game and these bitches were down here working. I know Ant wasn't a trick, but you still have some of these bitches who would fuck for practically nothing. This was my first year here, but hearing the stories what Tia shared with us made me shake my head. I put Ant's dick in my mouth and circled around his dick. I started sucking his dick slowly and taking my time. I relaxed my jaws and went further down taking all his dick in my mouth.

"Shit baby!" Ant said grabbing the back of my head.

I speeded up and sucked on the tip of his dick. I spit on it as my right hand jagged him off. I slurped and went back down deeper. Ant grabbed my hair and head again with both of his hands. My head bobbed up and down on his dick.

"Yes Kelly! I'm about to nut baby! You gonna swallow it baby?!" Ant asked.

I continued to suck his dick bobbing up and down. Ant shot his nut down my throat. I caught it, but didn't swallow it. I went to bathroom to spit it out. Ant hated when I did that, but I didn't care. I promised him that I will start swallowing it after we get married. I walked out the bedroom and my cell phone starting ringing. It was crazy Tia.

"Hey Tia, boo. What's good?" I said.

"Hey Kelly. I'm calling to tell you that all the girls are meeting at my room in about 30 minutes. I'm in room 222. I hope to see you soon," Tia said.

"That's cool, I will be there," I said.

284

"Tia where Tommy's ass at?" Ant asked in the background.

"He right here. Here Tommy, Ant wanna talk to you," Tia said.

I passed Ant my phone so that he could talk to Tommy. I went to go and slip on something comfortable. I put on a Juicy Couture jogging suit and some gym shoes. I wasn't about to walk around that big ass mall with heels on. Ant and Tommy was still talking on the food.

"Excuse me, but I hate to interrupt but can you call Tommy on your phone?" I said.

"Yeah, she want her phone back dude. Cool, I'm about to step out," Ant said.

He handed me phone back and his phone starting ringing. I kissed him good bye and waited till he got off the phone.

"I'm gone Ant. I will see you later. I love you and you better not be in any of these hoes face out here!" I said.

I got on the elevator and took it down to Tia's room. When I got there, Ciara and Neicy was already there.

"What's up ladies?! Let's do this shit!" I said excited.

"Are we going to invite, Aaliyah?" Neicy asked.

"Neicy don't nobody fuck with her like that," I said.

"We should invite her. She is up here too," Neicy said.

"Who the hell is Aaliyah?" Tia asked.

"Vell's girlfriend. The one I was telling you about whose cousin with the girl who ass Kelly and I beat when we was younger," Ciara said.

"Oh that girl, oh no she can't hang with us. I don't have time for no shady bitches around me," Tia said.

"Okay, I was just being nice," Neicy said.

"Girl, fuck being nice. Be you and everything will be just fine. Are you'll ready to go yet?" I said.

"Yeah let's go," Tia said.

We went to the mall and I was in awe. Wow, imagine if Chicago had a mall this damn big. "I will be shopping every day," I said.

"Girl, I will live in here," Ciara said.

We went to every store there was from Miu Miu, Neiman Marcus, BeBe, Gucci, Mac Cosmetics, and Victoria Secrets. I spent $2000 in Louis Vuitton. I saw a purse that I haven't seen in Chicago. Their prices were more reasonable than Chicago. Neicy and I decided to get our faces made up. Ciara and Tia remained shopping.

"Tia, I know we haven't really had a chance to talk. Well, I have something to tell you," I said.

"What's that Ciara?" Tia said.

"I got me a boo on the side," Ciara said.

"What! Are you serious? What's his name? Where he from? What does he do?" Tia asked smiling.

"Girl, his name is Kanye. He's lives in Chicago as well and he's an Architect," I said.

"Gone girl, I'm not mad at you. Smooth better get his shit together," Tia said.

"He trying to, but I just continue to me and act like that good girl that I've been. If he was doing his job, I wouldn't have to see anyone else. Kanye is different. He's mature and he makes me feel protective," I said.

"That's good as long as he treats you right that's all that matters. You know these men think and feel just because they have a little cash that we should accept and take everything that they do. You know I know that if Smooth was doing his part that you wouldn't being seeing another man. Do you boo because shit, I will cheat on Tommy's ass too if given the chance," Tia said.

"Tia is like I'm tired of making it work. But at the same time, I don't want to give up because of my family. You know how I feel about having a family because I didn't have that. That is why I forgive him when he fucked with Kayla and took him back when he had a child with Rochelle. Right now, I'm like I don't care and I'm going to do me. I know he's cheating on me now, but I don't really know with whom. Girl, I'm not even trying to search and look for it. If I find out then, I will go crazy," I said.

"If I were you, I wouldn't worry about it either. Why should you? Focus on the things that make you happy and that includes your new boo. Now, tell me more about Kanye the Architect. Does he have any cute friends?" Tia said.

Meanwhile

Denise and I was done getting our faces beat. We got our makeup done and out the way. Tia said that her sisters were coming to do our makeup, but Denise and I didn't want a rush job because she had so many faces to do. Tia understood that and she didn't get upset. Denise and I was walking through the mall to meet up with Ciara and Tia when we see Aaliyah. She was by herself carrying multiple shopping bags. I spotted her first, but didn't say anything. Aaliyah seen us and walked over to talk to us, well too Denise.

"Hey Neicy. Hi Kelly," Aaliyah said.

"Hey Aaliyah," Denise said.

"Hi," I said dry as hell.

"I see you guys have been doing some shopping. What party are you hitting up tonight? Maybe I can meet you there," Aaliyah said smiling.

"I'm not sure yet. There's so many parties going on. When I find out I will call and let you know," Denise said.

"Cool well, I'm going to do some more shopping. You guys have fun," Aaliyah said and walked off.

"Girl, she's not parting with me. If you want to party with her, you can but I'm cool," I said.

"HaHaHa! Kelly stop being mean you know that's your friend," Denise joked and said.

"Girl please, yeah ok. I don't trust the bitch. Never have and never will," I said.

We ran into Ciara and Tia and grabbed a quick bite to eat at Rain Forest Café before we headed back to the hotel.

Ebony

I rented a car and drove to Houston by myself. I asked the nail tech Cassandra if she wanted to come along and she said no. Oh well that didn't stop me because I was on a mission. I left Kimora in good hands with the baby sitter Stella. It was time for me to have some fun. I was hoping that I could come up tonight and find me a few niggas with money. It took me four hours to get to my destination. I had to get room and that weren't many rooms available so I stayed at the Days Inn. My room wasn't all that, but I didn't care because I didn't plan on being in the room. I planned on being out and having a good time. It was nine p.m. when I checked in my room. I wonder what party was popping tonight. On the ride here on the radio, I heard that 2 Chainz and Lil Wayne's party was the hottest ones. I didn't care for them and I really wanted to part with Puff Daddy and Jay Z. I know for sure it was going to be some money at one of those parties. I didn't care what party I got in as long as I partied. I know that it's going to be a lot of Chicago people here so I have to careful when I'm out and about. I got dressed and put on an all-white mini dress and pumps with gold accessories. Something simple. I didn't have to do too much because with a face and ass like mine I turn heads. I jumped in my rental and hit the strip where the parties were going to be. Every party was $200 and up to get into. I dipped into my cash that I had, but it was fine because I was going to replace it back. After driving around for forty minutes, I decided to go to Jeezy's party. I paid $500 to get in his party. I walked inside and that bitch was packed. There was women everywhere. Most of them bitches were busted and bodies were fucked up. Some were cute and had nice bodies. I didn't care about these hoes because I was the shit. As I walked through the crowd a lot of men looked and some grabbed . my hand. There was one guy that grabbed my arm.

"Damn Ma, you looking good tonight. Who you here with?" he said.

I looked him over and could see by the jewelry he was wearing that he had money. His chain, earrings, bracelet, watch, and pinky ring was blinding me. See it didn't take me long to get a nigga with cash. I spoke back.

"Hello and I'm here alone," I said smiling.

"Yeah, well what's your name?" he asked.

"My name is Red," I said lying. Rule number one you never give these niggas your real name when you hoeing, especially at an event like this because you don't know these people and who they know. Besides, he's not gonna give you his real name.

"Red that name does fit you. My name is Shorty. Why don't you join me and my people. We have a VIP section with unlimited drinks Ma," he said.

You see what I tell you. He gave me a fake name too. I laughed in my head and took him up on his offer.

"I would love to join you," I said smiling.

"Cool Ma follow me," Shorty said.

I followed Shorty through the crowd to where his section was. When I got there, it was men and women there. The ladies looked at me and rolled their eyes. They were mad and hating because I was the shit. I flipped my hair and shook my ass to Yo Gotti song, 'Act Right'. Shorty danced up on me and I grinded on him throwing my big ass back at him. My dress was coming up and I pulled it down because I didn't have on any panties. Shorty rubbed on my ass and

293

felt that I didn't have on any panties. "You leaving with me tonight, Red?" Shorty asked.

"If you got $600, I am," I said.

"I got it," he said pouring me some Champagne in a glass. This shit is too easy.

Ciara

Tommy had the connections to get us in Jeezy's party. We walked straight in and was seated in an exclusive area. I was happy with that because it was so people inside the building. If something jumped off, we were weren't down there in the crowd. It was me and Smooth, Tia and Tommy, Kelly and Ant, Denise and Red, and Aaliyah and Vell. We all sat down and the bartender bought over our bottles. I was happy to see that we had some Remy. Since I've tasted Remy at Denise's house, I fell in love with the taste. I sipped on a little and I saw Smooth watching me. He gave me a look and I caught it. Before we left the hotel, we had a talk and he told me that he didn't want me drinking. Being that we were out of town he didn't mind that I had one glass as long as he was around. I was sitting with the ladies. Me, Kelly, and Tia was talking. Denise and Aaliyah was talking as well.

"Tia, I see Tommy has a few connections," I said.

"Yes. I'm not trying to brag on my man and all, but Tommy is the man down here," Tia said.

"Girl please, it is fine if you brag about your man, but only to us," Kelly said laughing.

"I'm loving Texas. Everything here is big," I said.

"Yes and you guys have to come back and visit me in Dallas. I want you to meet my mother and my sisters," Tia said.

"You know when Smooth flying here I'm on that plane with his ass," I said.

"Me too. Ant said that he will be doing a lot of trips down here. Oh shit! That's my song!" Kelly said.

Kelly jumped up and start dancing to Yo Gotti song, 'Act Right.' Tia and I continued to talk as Kelly walked over and started dancing with Ant.

"Have you heard from Kanye?" Tia asked sipping on her drink.

"Yes, I stuck and talked to him while I was in the shower. Besides, that we have been texting each other back to back like crazy," I said.

"Be careful and erase your messages. You never know if he goes through your phone," Tia said.

"I do all the time," I said.

During our conversation, I received a text message from Kanye. I responded back letting him know that I was out and that I would call him tomorrow. He was cool with that. I was at the party with Smooth and I didn't want to risk getting caught up texting another man. Kanye keeps asking me to fly to California next week. I want to pull it and sneak off and fly to California, but what was I going to tell Smooth. I eased my mind and started to enjoy the party. I noticed that it was a lot of women in this party naked. One girl had on a see through dress and she left little to the imagination. I could see one girl had her eye on Smooth and I jumped up and starting dancing with him. The girl backed off and went on searching for her victim. Smooth had on his ice looking good. My babe got fresh for Houston. He looked so good that I had to tell him.

"Babe, you look so fine," I whispered in his ear.

"You look so sexy. I can't wait to get back to the hotel and fuck the shit out of you," Smooth said.

"I love it when you talk dirty to me," I said.

I was about to say something back until I heard an altercation going on behind me.

"Bitch, you better get the fuck out of Vell's face! What the fuck is you on?! Are you fucking my man?!" Aaliyah said to some girl.

"Vell you better get your girl!" the girl said rolling her eyes and walking away.

"Chill out bae. I'm not fucking that girl!" Vell said.

"Don't mutherfucking tell me to chill out! Vell, you must think that I'm stupid!" Aaliyah said.

Aaliyah stormed out of the party. Vell stayed there with the rest of us. I shook my head and told Vell to go after her. Vell didn't want to leave the party, but he went after her. As soon as he left, Kelly and the girls filled me in on what had happened.

Ebony

I was still chilling with Shorty and his people. It was getting late and I was tipsy and horny. Shorty couldn't keep his hands off me. I was feeling him up also he had a nice sized dick. I also felt the money inside all of his pockets. Yes Shorty was getting this pussy tonight. He was feeling on my ass as I poked it out dancing to the music. You would've thought that we were both a couple. His people told him that they were ready to leave. I was ready to leave too. We walked through the crowd and Shorty had his arms wrapped around me. We made it outside.

"Red follow me back to my room. You ready for the after party?" Shorty asked.

"Yes I am. I'm following you," I said.

I made it to my car and fought the traffic. For a minute, I didn't see Shorty and I called him and he told me to meet him at the hotel. I made it to Shorty's room. He opened the door and I stepped inside. It was him and two of the guys that were at the party with him. I already knew what was up, but I played dumb.

"What's Shorty?" I asked.

"All three of us want to fuck you. How much for a foursome?" Shorty asked.

"It will be $600 a piece for the three of you," I said.

The guys pulled out their money. I collected the money and took off my dress.

"Damn!" One of the guys said.

We drank and smoked weed. I was ready for that action. Shorty pulled out some condoms and all three of them put them on. I walked over to Shorty and dropped to my knees. He pulled down his pants and I sucked his dick. Both his friends walked over and pulled their pants down. I was lucky that they all had average sized dicks. My night was going to be an easy one. I sucked on each of their dicks one by one as I remained on my knees. The other two got undressed and one guy laid down. I straddled the one who was lying on the floor and bounced up and down on his dick. I sucked and licked Shorty and his friend's dick at the same time. The one who I was fucking grabbed me by my waist slamming his pole inside of me deeper.

"Oh shit! Yes!" I moaned.

"This hoe got some good pussy," the guy said.

"I want that ass," Shorty said.

We switched up and I started fucking the third guy. Shorty fucked me in my ass as I sucked the second guy dick standing in front of me.

"Mmmmmm! Mmmmmm! Yes Shorty fuck my ass!" I said.

He pulled me by my hair. "You like this dick?! You like getting fucked in your ass?!" Shorty said fucking me.

"Yes, I love your dick in my ass! Mmmmmm!" I said.

The second guy pushed my head further down on his dick causing me to gag. I had three dicks in all three holes and this shit felt good. What a great way to start back having sex. The third guy I was fucking actually had the best dick. He was filling my pussy up and I creamed all over his dick.

"Yesssss, your dick feels good in my pussy. Yessssssssss! Oh yes fuck me!" I said.

Shorty and the third guy fucked the shit out of me. The second guy wanted to feel what my asshole was like so Shorty gave him the chance to hit it.

"Oh shit this is some good ass!" The second guy said.

I was now on top of him and Shorty had both of my legs in the air fucking the shit out me. The third guy fucked my mouth. I looked him as he filled my mouth with dick. I swallowed his dick up. He pumped in and out my mouth. Shorty pumped in and out my pussy. The second guy pumped in and out my ass.

"Damn, I'm about to nut! Red, you got some good pussy! Your hoe ass got it!" Shorty said pumping faster.

"Ohhhhh! Ohhhhh!" I moaned as three of them fucked me faster.

"Shit oh shit!" The second guy said.

He pushed me off his dick and pulled off his condom. Shorty and the third guy pulled theirs off as well. They stroked their dicks over me as I fingered my pussy about to cum again for the second time. Shorty shot his nut first on me.

"Shitttttt!" Shorty said.

The other two shot their nut on me right after.

"Yessssss!" I moaned as I creamed all over my fingers.

"You a freaky hoe!" Shorty said smiling.

I got up and grabbed my purse and dress and went to the washroom to clean myself up. I would shower once I got back to my hotel. I made my money and went my hoe ass back to my hotel. I was loving All-Star Weekend.

Vell

"Damn Aaliyah, why are you packing? You not leaving and going anywhere!" I said.

"Vell, you think I'm dumb. I know that you're fucking that bitch next door," Aaliyah said.

"Look, I'm not fucking her and I'm getting tired of telling you that!" I said.

"What a coincidence that she is in the same party as you. We all the way in Houston and this bitch still manages to bump into you! You must think that I'm stupid!" Aaliyah said.

"Look Aaliyah, everyone from the Chi is down here. I can't help if she seen me in a fucking party. Calm down and relax. You not going anywhere," I said.

I started kissing on her. Aaliyah tried to push me off of her, but I continued to kiss her.

"I love you so stop tripping and shit. We out of town and I want you to stay her and enjoy it," I said.

Aaliyah didn't say anything as I kissed her. I pulled off her dress. She cried, but didn't stop me from caressing her. I pulled her panties to the side and slid inside of her. Aaliyah gasped as I pumped my dick in her. She eased up and kissed me back.

"I don't want to fight. I don't want to make you cry," I said.

"I don't want to fight either," Aaliyah said.

"You know how much I love you. You're the only one," I said.

"Oh yes Vell! I love you too," Aaliyah said.

I fucked the shit out of Aaliyah and put her to sleep. Damn, I can't believe that she seen Victoria aka Vicky. I was hoping that they didn't run into each other. Yes I'm fucking Vicky my next door neighbor. Shit Vicky was bad and had too much ass for me to pass up. I didn't have plans on fucking her in the beginning, but she kept on throwing me the pussy so I gave it a try. Needless to say, she had a hook and we didn't stop fucking. We've been creeping four two months now. Vicky was a sweet woman who knows how to cater to a man. She does everything that I tell her to do without a problem. Aaliyah is my love, but she complains and nags too damn much. Since the first day that I've met her, she has always been that way. I still give her what she asks for. She doesn't have to work and I provide for my family. Still at the end of it, all she finds something to complain about. When I'm with Vicky, its peaceful that's why when she asked me to pay for her trip to Houston I didn't have a problem with it. I knew that she was down here, but I didn't think that with so many people here that we would bump into each other. My phone vibrated and it was Vicky texting me: Hey bae. I'm back at the hotel now. I miss you.

Cool and I miss you too. I texted back.

Can u come through?' Vicky texted.

No. I will hit you tomorrow. I texted.

Ok see you tomorrow. Vicky texted.

I turned my phone off and rolled over and wrapped my arms around Aaliyah and went to sleep.

The next was here and Aaliyah wouldn't let me out of her sight. We had brunch at Cheesecake Factory and afterwards we shopped. I had to meet up with the fellas this evening and I was hoping that I would be able to dip off with Vicky before or after. There was no way that I would be able to spend the night with her. Aaliyah was glued to my fucking hip. While we were shopping, Vicky texted me. When I tried to hit her back, Aaliyah's eyes was watching me. I was so happy when we bumped into Red and Denise.

"What's Red? Hey Denise. I see ya'll doing some shopping," I said.

"What up Aaliyah? Hell yeah, boy we getting a few things," Red said.

Aaliyah and Denise was off to the side talking. It was my chance to tell Red what the hell was going on.

"Damn man, Aaliyah won't let me breathe. I can't even take a piss without her holding my dick," I said.

"Man bro. That shit was crazy last night. Did Vicky know that you were at Jeezy party?" Red asked.

"Come on man. You know me better than that. Hell nawl, I would never have the both of them in the same fucking party. I need you to help me shake her," I said.

"I got you bro," Red said laughing.

Denise and Aaliyah walked back over to us smiling.

"Hey Red is it fine if I go off with Aaliyah and have some girl time?" Denise asked.

I looked at Red now was the time to save me.

"Damn baby, you gonna leave me. It's cool you can chill with Aaliyah," Red said laughing.

"Baby, I will meet the back at the room before you leave to meet up with the fellas," Aaliyah said kissing me.

"Cool bae and enjoy yourself," I said kissing her back.

The two of them walked off. I was free and I texted Vicky and told her that I will be there in twenty minutes.

I knocked on Vicky's hotel door. She answered the door naked. I smacked her on her bubble ass.

"We have to hurry up. I don't have much time," I said.

Vicky undressed me and started licking my dick and balls.

"I'm sorry about last night daddy. I didn't mean to get you in any trouble," Vicky said apologizing to my dick.

My dick jumped and she gobbled it up. I covered my face with the pillow. Her head game was serious.

"Shit girl!" I said grabbing her head with both of my hands.

Vicky slurped and slobbed on my dick.

"Turn around!" I said.

She turned around so that I could see her phat ass in the air. I fucked her from the back and her ass wiggled and jiggled. I rubbed and smacked her across the ass.

"Yes Vell, hit that shit!" Vicky moaned.

"Look at me! Kiss me! Tell me whose pussy is this!" I said pumping in her.

Vicky looked back at me and kissed me. "This your pussy Vell! All yours Vell!" Vicky said.

"I'm about to nut Vicky! Oh I love fucking you!" I said.

"I love it when you fuck me Vell," Vicky said.

"Urgggggggggg!" I moaned loudly releasing my stress and nut.

I shook a few more times before I got up to wash my dick off. Vicky rolled over on her back and smiled. I walked out the bathroom.

"Aye, we can't speak to each other when we see one another," I said.

"Okay that's fine with me. I didn't even see her. If I knew she was there, I would've kept on walking and acted like I didn't even see you," Vicky said.

"I know that you didn't baby," I said putting on my clothes.

"I wish that you didn't have to go so fast. You promise me that we would spend some time together down here," Vicky said.

"I don't want to leave either. I will take you out to eat tonight. You just be ready when I call you," I said.

"Okay I will," Vicky said.

"Alright I'm gone. Here goes a little something," I said kissing her and giving her some money.

"Thank you Vell and see you tonight," Vicky said.

I made it back to the room before Aaliyah got there. I jumped in the shower and when I got out she was coming through the door.

Chapter Nineteen

Ciara

It has been a week since we've back home from Houston. Things were back to normal and I was still seeing Kanye. I had a date with him today and I was excited. I was spending time with the children and we were at Enchanted Castle. Kelly tagged along because Smooth had to handle some business. The children played and Junior was growing up so fast and looking like his father. Erica showed her little brother how to play the game and I thought it was so cute. I snapped a picture and sent it off to Smooth. He replied back saying how he wished that he was here with us. Kelly and I was eating the nasty pizza and talking.

"So have you found out where Kanye was taking you?" Kelly asked me.

"No he will not tell me. I really want to know. He always like surprising me," I said.

"I think it is sweet. Ciara, do you plan on sneaking and continuing seeing him?"

"I've thought about. He has asked me to be his girl and only his girl. I don't know right now. I'm just enjoying myself. We haven't had sex or he isn't pressuring me to have sex. I still have to get to know him. Right now, I'm just going with the flow," I said.

"I feel you. Enjoy yourself and have fun. Smooth had his fun and did his thing. I don't blame you," Kelly said.

"I'm not seeing Kanye to get back at Smooth. I'm just doing it because I'm bored with Smooth and the relationship. The trust and the loyalty is gone. He being cool now, but I don't know. Every time I try to leave something keep holding me back. I don't know what the hell I'm doing Kelly," I said.

"Girl, it's okay for you to feel that way. I felt the same exact way last year dealing with Ant. I prayed about it. There was so many times when I was ready to leave Ant and didn't trust him because of his actions," Kelly said.

"I know that shit was crazy last year. I can't believe that Ebony had set him up. Plus, how Rochelle trying to kill me. We been through so much shit that we could write a book," I said.

"Hahaha that's a good idea. I might just do that. Lord knows I have a lot to write about from my childhood until now," Kelly said.

"I'm sorry, I've been meaning to ask you how is your mother?" I asked.

"She's doing fine. She's up for an appeal soon. I really hope that she gets out. I miss my mom very much and I hate seeing her locked up," Kelly said.

"I'm blessed that my mom has gotten help with her addiction. I know I said that I was going to see someone, but I haven't been really drinking a lot like I've used to. I guess meeting Kanye has helped me cope with that," I said.

"You made me so upset with you. Do you remember in Houston when we were in the party you start singing, 'If the Remy's in the system.' Ciara you was drunk then."

"Girl yes, and I only had one drink. Smooth and I got back to the hotel and he beat the pussy up that night. Kelly, I was like damn is this Smooth," I said laughing.

"I know Ant put it down too when we were there. Ciara do you swallow Smooth's nut? Ant keeps on pressuring me to swallow his," Kelly said.

"Yes, I have plenty of times. At first, it was nasty, but after a while I got used to the taste. Girl, you better swallow Ant's nut you around walking with a ring on your finger," I said.

"I'm so lame Ciara. I need to step my head game up," Kelly laughed and said.

"Why don't you watch porn? That's how I learned," I said.

"I think that would be better because I am a visual person. The lady was good at Denise's party, but I needed more time," Kelly said.

"Yes, she was excellent. I tried that grapefruit trick on Smooth and he loved it," I said.

"You did Ciara. Hahaha, I have to try it on Ant," Kelly said.

Kelly and I walked over to play with the kids. Junior was crazy about Auntie Kelly. He kept on pulling her from game to game so that she could play with him. I laughed and played with Erica. Let me find out that Junior has a crush on Kelly.

Later that night, I met Kanye for my date. It was at the Improv in Schaumburg at Woodfield Mall. I thought the date was cool. The comedian was funny and I laughed all night. They had really good food and strong drinks. I told Smooth that I was with London hanging out. He seemed fine with that. It was funny because before I left out Smooth said that we needed to start going back out more. I agreed and kissed him before I left out the door. I was sitting there and thinking about Smooth while I was on a date with Kanye. I guess I was starting to feel a little guilty about being here. The more I drank the less I felt the guilt. I had four drinks and that was my limit for the night. I was tipsy, but was still aware of what I was doing. The show was over and I excused myself to go the washroom. I went to pee and after that I brushed my teeth so that I could have minty fresh breath. When I stepped out, Kanye was waiting for me.

"Did you enjoy yourself tonight beautiful?" Kanye asked.

"Yes I did. It was a great show. I haven't laughed like that in so long," I said.

"I'm happy that you had a really good time," Kanye said.

We walked back to our cars. I was leaning against my car as Kanye and I started to kiss. It was cold outside and little snowflakes started to fall. I stopped kissing Kanye to sneeze.

"Achooo! Achooo!" I sneezed twice.

"Bless you. Get inside and call me once you make it home beautiful," Kanye said.

I got inside my car and closed the door.

"I had a great time and I will call you once I make it home. You be safe too," I said and rolled off.

March

Cherish

I went into labor and I had to be rushed to the County hospital. My umbilical cord was wrapped around my baby's neck. The doctors had to perform an emergency Cesarean Section. They numbed me up and did the operation fast. They covered the lower part of my body so that I didn't see what was going on. Once they pulled my baby out, she was bluish and wasn't making a sound. The two continued to perform surgery on me while the other two rushed my baby off to the side.

"What's wrong with baby?!" I cried.

The doctors ignored me and they performed CPR on my baby. I was hand cuffed to the bed.

"What's wrong with my fucking baby?!" I yelled again.

"Calm down." The officer said.

"You tell me to calm the fuck down! Why is my baby blue? Why isn't my baby crying?!" I yelled.

I tried to get out of the bed, but one of my hands was cuffed to the bed. I couldn't feel the bottom part of my body because of the epidural. The doctors were working on my baby then I finally heard her cry.

"Waa, Waa, Waa!" My baby cried.

I started crying. "Can I hold my baby, please?

The doctors bought my baby over to me.

"Thank you God for allowing my baby to make it. Hey pretty. Hey Laniyah you scared me princess," I said.

The doctors took my daughter away.

"Can I please hold her a little longer? Please don't take her away," I said.

The guards told me to relax and the doctors took my baby off. I knew that they had to do it, but I wasn't expecting them to do it so soon. They pushed me to my room. I cried as they rolled me down the hall. People looked at me, but I didn't care. Once I got to my room, I felt a lot better. I asked for an extra sheet because I was cold. All the medication that I was on made me fall asleep.

Two Hours Later

I woke up and the guard was sitting there watching television. He pressed the nurse button and she came inside.

"Hello Cherish, how are you? My name is Kesha and I will be you nurse for today," she said.

"I'm fine. Kesha, where is my baby?" I said.

Kesha took my vital signs and asked me a series of questions and checked them off.

"Cherish, a social worker will be in here to talk to you soon."

She lifted up my gown to exam my Cesarean Section. The guard looked away and I was thankful for that. Even though I had my rights taken away, he still respected me enough to give me a little privacy. She changed the gauze from my surgery.

"Cherish you have dissolvable staples. They usually take around 6 weeks to dissolve. Are you in any pain?" Nurse Kesha asked.

"Yes I am. Right where the incision is. I also have a migraine headache. My head is banging," I said.

"I will bring you some pain medicine," Kesha said.

She left out the door. I turned the television on to watch Maury. A white woman walked in my room carrying a folder.

"Good Morning Cherish. My name is Mrs. Peterson and I am with the Department of Corrections. I am here so that you can sign your paperwork for the release of your baby. You do understand that you have to return back to jail and your baby goes to whomever you are signing her too. It says here on the paper that the father Lorenzo Jones is the parent that is taking the baby into custody," Mrs. Peterson said.

"Yes I granted him custody of baby until I get there," I said.

"Great. Lorenzo Jones is here now and ready to take your baby home. I just need you to sign these papers and your baby will be released to the legal guardian," Mrs. Peterson said.

I signed the papers and Mrs. Peterson left out the room. I asked the guard if I could make a phone and he allowed me. I called Lorenzo.

"Hey baby. How are you? I'm here now in the hospital getting Laniyah," Lorenzo said.

"I'm fine and I know the social worker just left. Thank you for coming to get her. I love you," I said.

"You don't have to thank me. This is my baby so I'm doing what a father is supposed to do. I love you and I'm going to make sure that our princess is going to be taken care of," Lorenzo said.

"Okay, I will call you back later. Make sure that you call my mom and tell her the news. Kiss my baby for me," I said.

I hung up the phone. I had three and a half months to go and I will be out this bitch. I'm happy that I had a healthy baby girl. July needs to hurry up and get here.

April

Kayla

"Push! Push! I need one good last push!" the doctor said.

"Ugggggg! Ugggggg!" I pushed my baby out as I was hand cuffed to the bed.

"Waaaa! Waaaa! Waaaaa!" My baby cried.

"My baby. Can I hold her, please? Can you please take off these cuffs?" I said.

"No Ms., we cannot remove the handcuffs," the officer said.

The nurse held my baby in front of me.

"Hey my precious baby," I said talking to my baby girl.

"What would you like to name her?" the nurse asked.

"Variyah Jackson," I said to the nurse as I looked at my baby.

CPSIA information can be obtained
at www.ICGtesting.com
Printed in the USA
LVOW04s1749021216
515533LV00010B/944/P